AMAL UNBOUND

Also by Aisha Saeed

Written in the Stars

AMAL UNBOUND

Aisha Saeed

Nancy Paulsen Books

NANCY PAULSEN BOOKS
an imprint of Penguin Random House LLC
375 Hudson Street
New York, NY 10014

Library of Congress Cataloging-in-Publication Data
Names: Saeed, Aisha, author.
Title: Amal unbound / Aisha Saeed.
Description: New York, NY : Nancy Paulsen Books, [2018]
Summary: In Pakistan, Amal holds on to her dream of being a
teacher even after becoming an indentured servant to pay off
her family's debt to the wealthy and corrupt Khan family.
Identifiers: LCCN 2017038160 | ISBN 9780399544682 (hardback : alk. paper)
ISBN 9780399544705 (ebook)
Subjects: | CYAC: Indentured servants—Fiction.
Family life—Pakistan—Fiction. | Courage—Fiction. | Comduct of life—Fiction.
Pakistan—Fiction. | BISAC: JUVENILE FICTION / Family / General (see also headings under
Social Issues). JUVENILE FICTION / People & Places / Middle East. JUVENILE FICTION /
Social Issues / General (see also headings under Family).
Classification: LCC PZ7.1.S24 Am 2018 | DDC [Fic]—dc23
LC record available at https://lccn.loc.gov/2017038160

Printed in the United States of America.
ISBN 9780399544682
3 5 7 9 10 8 6 4

Design by Dave Kopka. Text set in Stone Seri ITC Std.

For Ami and Abu, my first teachers.

Chapter 1

I watched from the window as the boys tumbled out of the brick schoolhouse across the field from us. Our class was running over. Again.

Girls shifted in their seats and sneaked glances at the clock above the chalkboard. My friend Hafsa sighed.

"And finally, I have some bad news," Miss Sadia told us. She picked up a stack of papers from her desk. "I finished grading your math tests. Only five of you passed."

The class let out a collective groan.

"Now, now," she hushed us. "This just means we have more work to do. We'll go over it tomorrow and take another test next week."

"Those questions were hard," my younger sister Seema

whispered to me. We lined up by the chalkboard at the front of the class to get our tests. "I should've stayed with the younger class until fall."

"Oh, come on. You know you probably passed," I whispered back. "When have you ever failed an exam?"

Seema tugged at her sleeves as she walked up to Miss Sadia. It was only in the arms that you could see my old uniform was too big on her. Miss Sadia handed Seema the paper. As expected, Seema's worried expression shifted to a smile. Her steps were lighter before she slipped out of the classroom.

"I'm sorry I can't help today," I told Miss Sadia once the room was empty. This was my favorite part of the day, when everyone left and it was just the two of us. The building felt like it had exhaled, expanding a little bit without all thirty-four of us, crammed two to a desk, filling up nearly every square inch of space. "My mother is in bed again."

"Is the baby almost here?"

"Yes, so my father said I have to come home and watch my sisters."

"I'll miss your help, Amal, but he's right; family comes first."

I knew helping family was what a good eldest daughter did, but this time after school with Miss Sadia wasn't just fun; it was important. I wanted to be a teacher when I grew up, and who better to learn from than the best teacher I ever had? I loved washing the chalkboards, sweeping the floor, and hearing stories of her college days. I loved watching her go over her lessons and rework them based on what worked and what didn't the day before. I learned so much from watching her. How could my father not understand?

"I could still use your help with the poetry unit next week," she told me. "Some of the students are grumbling about it. Think you could convince Hafsa to give it a chance? You know how she rallies the others to her side. She'll listen to you."

"I don't think she minds reading the poems. Writing them makes her nervous."

"You'd think everyone would be happy to write poetry! Shorter than an essay."

"It's different. The great poets like Ghalib, Rumi, Iqbal—they had things to say."

"And don't you have things to say?"

"What would I write about?" I laughed. "My little sisters? My father's sugarcane fields and orange groves? I love *reading* poems, but there's nothing for me to really write about. Our life is boring."

"That's not true! Write about what you see! Write about your dreams. Pakistan was founded by the dreams of poets. Aren't we of the same earth?"

Miss Sadia's dramatic way of talking was one of the reasons I loved her, but I wasn't convinced. It's not that I wasn't proud of my family and our life. I was lucky to belong to one of the more prosperous families in our Punjabi village, but it didn't change the fact that I lived in a village so tiny, it didn't even register as a dot on a map.

But I promised I'd talk to Hafsa.

This is what I now remember most about my last afternoon at school—the smell of the dusty chalkboard, the sound of the students lingering outside the door, and, mostly, how easily I took my ordinary life for granted.

Chapter 2

I raced down the school's gravel walkway to catch up to Seema and Hafsa. The sun blazed overhead, warming my chador and my hair beneath it.

"I'm buying Miss Sadia one of those bells I see on TV. You know, the kind that rings when class is over?" Hafsa grumbled.

"She doesn't always keep us late," I protested.

"Remember last week?" Hafsa said. "How she went on and on about constellations? By the time I got home, my brothers were out of their school clothes and halfway through their homework."

"But wasn't it interesting?" I asked. "The way the night

stars help us when we're lost and tell all sorts of different stories?"

"Why do I need to know about connecting dots in the sky? I want to be the first doctor in my family. Not the first astronaut," Hafsa said.

Hafsa and I had been friends so long, I couldn't remember a time I didn't know her, but when she talked like this, I didn't understand her at all. Unlike Hafsa, I wanted to know everything there was to know. How fast did airplanes fly? Why did some leave whiffs of clouds in their wake and others didn't? Where did ladybugs go when the rain came hard and fast? What was it like to walk through the streets of Paris or New York or Karachi? There was so much I didn't know that even if I spent my whole life trying, I knew I could only learn a small percentage of it.

"How's your mom?" Hafsa asked. "My mother said her back is hurting."

"It's gotten worse," I told her. "She couldn't get out of bed yesterday."

"My mother said that's a good sign. Backaches mean a boy," Hafsa said. "I know that would make your parents happy."

"It would be fun to have a brother," I said.

"There it is! Look at the door!" Hafsa said when we turned the bend toward our homes. She pointed to the building that had appeared next to our village mosque. A structure had never emerged quite like this before with no explanation. Two weeks ago, a concrete foundation had been poured onto the field where we played soccer. The next week, brick walls arose and windows appeared, and today there was a door—painted lime green!

"Any idea yet what it could be?" I asked her.

"Yes." Hafsa grinned. If Hafsa could have it her way, she'd be permanently stationed by the crates of fruit at her family's market, soaking up every bit of gossip. "Khan Sahib is building a factory."

I rolled my eyes. Rumors and gossip were a part of life in our village. Some of the talk was ordinary, about the state of the crops or the weather, but often it centered on Khan Sahib, our village's powerful landlord.

"Why would he build a factory here? He has plenty in Islamabad and Lahore," Seema said. "What we need is a clinic. Look how much Amma's back hurts. The doctor in town is good, but this village needs a proper clinic."

"Do you really think Khan Sahib would put up anything to help us?" Hafsa scoffed.

"Maybe it's not him building it," I suggested.

"Look at the fancy green door! Who else has time and money to waste like that? You know I'm right."

Any unexplainable situation was always pinned to

Khan Sahib. He was the mysterious figure I'd heard of all my life but never seen. When I was younger, he loomed large and scary, like a character in a horror story.

"Sure! He's the one who breathes fire when he talks, right?" I rolled my eyes.

"Didn't he pick all the fruit off Naima's guava tree?" Seema winked.

"I heard he's why we've had no rain for months," I continued.

"I don't decide what I hear," Hafsa huffed. "I just report it."

"We'll find out what it is soon enough." I hooked my arm through Seema's. "But in the meantime, let's hope it's a clinic."

Hafsa's house came first on our path, just past the post office. Then came mine. I saw it in the distance. Gray like the others surrounding it except for the roses my mother planted around its border just before I was born; they still bloomed each spring around this time, without fail. It's why spring was my favorite time of year.

My friend Omar pedaled past us in his blue and khaki school uniform. He chimed his bell three times, our signal to meet. The stream. That's the direction he was headed in.

"Oh no." I looked in my book bag. "I left my exam in class."

"Again?" Hafsa frowned.

"Tell Amma I won't be long?" I asked Seema.

Seema hesitated. Our father would be home soon, but she knew Omar didn't chime his bicycle bell three times unless it was important.

"Okay." Seema nodded. "Hurry."

Chapter 3

Omar waited for me by the narrow stream that sliced through the length of our village. This was one of our usual spots, the wooded area next to my father's fields where our towering green stalks of sugarcane met the orange groves that dotted the landscape into the horizon. This area was far enough from the heart of the fields where our workers spent most of their time fertilizing the earth and keeping the groves and stalks trimmed and cared for, but even if they ventured to the edges, the shade trees here were thick and leafy, shielding us from view.

"I brought it!" he said when I approached and sat next to him on the fallen tree bridging the stream. He handed me a book with a burnt-orange cover.

I ran my hands over the raised lettering. The complete works of Hafiz. We had a small collection of books in our class, but it was no secret that the boys' school had a much bigger library to choose from.

"So, what did you think?" I asked him. "Which one was your favorite poem?"

"Favorite?" He frowned.

"Omar!" I exclaimed. "You didn't even read one poem?"

"I bring you what you like. Doesn't mean I have to read it."

"Yes, you do." I poked him. "I need someone to talk about it with."

"Fine," he said, raising his hands in surrender. "I'll read some after you're done. That's how good of a friend I am."

Omar's dark hair looked almost brown under the bright afternoon sun. Looking at him, it hit me yet again how unfair it was for God to give me a friend who understood me completely and create him as a boy.

"Amal, I know he's your friend, but you're not a little girl anymore," my mother had lectured me a few months ago when I turned twelve. "You can't spend so much time with him."

"But he's like our brother," I had protested. "How can I not see him?"

"Of course you'll see him around the house—some

11

conversations can't be avoided—but walking to school together, talking freely the way you both do . . . people will start gossiping if they aren't already."

Omar and I were born three days apart. He lived with his mother, our servant Parvin, in the shed behind our house. They moved there after his father died, and I'd never known life without him. He was part of the fabric of who I was. I couldn't follow this rule. Neither could Omar. So now we met in secret to talk, to listen to each other, to laugh.

"I told Miss Sadia I wouldn't be able to stay after school," I said. "I'm hoping it's just until the baby comes, but my father said we'll have to see how it goes."

"Once things settle down, he'll change his mind."

"I hope you're right," I said.

"Your father probably got fed up because Safa unlatched a neighbor's chicken coop again. You know you're the only one who can keep up with her."

"Omar, she did not!" I tried to stay serious, but a smile escaped. My youngest sister *was* a constant source of drama in our house.

"See? You know I'm right. Your poor father probably spent the morning chasing chickens and apologizing to neighbors."

"You need to stop with the Safa conspiracies all the time." I told him.

"Ha!" He grinned. "I'm going to have to become a lawyer. Safa will need a team of them with the trouble she gets into."

"She's only three!" I swatted him, but just like that, some of the heaviness lifted. He was right. Besides, my father usually gave in to us if we pleaded enough.

"Speaking of school, the headmaster from Ghalib Academy called. I got in!"

"Omar!" I exclaimed. "I knew it! Didn't I say so?"

"And they're going to cover everything! Room and board, all of it! This could change everything for me, Amal. If I do well enough, I could get one of their college scholarships. Can you believe it? Maybe I'll even get my mother her own house one day."

I hugged him. Omar had been attending the school across from mine, but Ghalib was one of the best schools around, a boys' boarding school a few towns over. Attending it was a lucky break for a servant's son like Omar. He was right—it could truly change everything for him.

"I wonder what the library there is like," I said.

"That was fast." He laughed. "Can I settle in to the school first before you have me hunting down books for you?"

"No way!" I said. "But I bet they'll have more books than both our classrooms combined. And Hafsa told me some boarding schools have cafeterias with all the food you can eat and televisions in all the bedrooms."

"I don't know about that," he said. "But they do have an after-school chess club and a debate team. And the dorm has a computer lab we can use in our spare time. The only thing is I'll have to share a room with another student. Maybe even two students."

"Do you know who they'll be?"

"No. I'll meet them when I go there for orientation weekend, but it'll be strange living with people I don't know."

"Hafsa's already staked her claim on me to be her roommate when we go to college someday."

"Well, at least with Hafsa as a roommate, you'll be up to date on all the inside information about everyone and everything on campus."

"That's definitely a plus." I laughed.

The clink of glass bracelets shattered our solitude.

It was Seema. She ran toward us, her feet bare.

"Come quick," she said between gasps of breath. "The baby is coming."

Chapter 4

The five minutes it took to run to my home on the other side of the field felt like a lifetime. We zigzagged through the sugarcane, taking shortcuts through the maze we knew so well. Our feet crunched over twigs and fallen leaves until we tumbled into the clearing that led to my house.

Flinging open the front door, I raced through our living room and straight into my parents' bedroom. My mother lay in bed. A thin sheet was draped over her. Raheela Bibi, the midwife, pressed a damp towel to her forehead. My mother's eyes were shut. Her jaw clenched.

"But this wasn't supposed to happen for another few weeks!" I said.

"Well, it's happening now!" Raheela Bibi rummaged through her bag.

My mother exhaled and opened her eyes. She looked at me. Her cheeks were flushed and her forehead was pale.

"Amal," she said. "You shouldn't be in here."

It was true; unmarried girls, especially my age, weren't allowed in the birthing area. But how could I stay outside when something was obviously wrong?

"I'm worried," I told her.

"I'm fine," she said. "Babies come early all the time." She smiled at me, but her eyes didn't crinkle with the up-turn of her lips. She patted my arm and moved to say more, but suddenly she gasped and clenched her jaw again.

"I'm here." I squeezed her hand.

A hand touched my elbow. Omar's mother, Parvin, had arrived. Wisps of black hair framed her face from beneath her chador.

"Amal, I can stay with her now," Parvin told me. "Will you go take care of Safa and Rabia?"

"But I want to help."

"Taking care of your little sisters is helping. It gives your mother one less thing to worry about."

I wanted to stay, but she was right. And it was too hard seeing my mother like this.

I stepped into our living room. Rabia and Safa stood stock-still in their cotton frocks next to the faded sofa.

"Is Amma okay?" Rabia asked. Her lower lip quivered. Safa bit her nails and said nothing. Rabia was four years old and Safa was three, but with their matching black curls and dimples, people often mistook them for twins.

"Of course she's fine." I pushed down my own fear and ran a hand through Rabia's springy hair. "The baby is coming. Aren't you excited to meet your new brother or sister?"

They glanced at each other and then nodded at me.

"Let's go in your bedroom and dress up your dolls while we wait. We can show them to the baby soon."

Both girls followed me into their bedroom next to the kitchen. Their window overlooked our courtyard, the concrete floor painted peach, where our mother cooked meals when the weather allowed. Safa and Rabia pulled out their dolls and the collection of clothes my mother sewed for them. Soon they were chatting and giggling and getting their dolls ready for a tea party.

I tried to focus on their play and push out the image of my mother's closed eyes and pained face. I knew people kept saying they hoped the baby was a boy, but right now I didn't care. I only wanted my mother to be okay.

The door creaked. Omar stood by the edge of the bedroom, his hand resting on the knob.

"How's she doing?" he asked.

"I don't know. I was only in there with her for a few minutes. But it was scary—she looked so weak."

"Raheela Bibi and my mother know what they're doing," Omar tried to reassure me. "And you are right here if they need you."

"The book!" I turned to him. "I left it by the stream. We ran so fast, I forgot all about it."

"Don't worry about the book."

"It looked expensive."

"I'll get it. It's not going anywhere."

"What if something happens to her?" My voice cracked.

"We don't know anything yet," he said. "But don't worry; I'll be here if *you* need me."

I appreciated his words because he did not promise me all would be well. He did not know.

Neither did I.

Chapter 5

My father paced the length of the living room in his leather sandals while my sister and I sat at the table by the sofa, trying to do our homework. His forehead was slick with sweat; his dark glasses framed his worried expression.

We had a bigger house than many, but right now it felt like it was shrinking in on me. Seema and I kept stealing glances at our parents' closed room while our little sisters played in their bedroom.

The sun had nearly set when my parents' bedroom door finally opened.

The midwife stepped outside and smiled.

My jaw unclenched. My mother was okay. She had to be if Raheela Bibi was smiling.

"Congratulations," she said. "You are a father five times over now."

"How is Mehnaz?" he asked.

"Tired. But she'll be fine. Go on in and see for yourself."

My father walked into the bedroom. Seema and I followed.

The lamp on the nightstand lent a soft glow to the darkened room. The little one, smaller than I expected, lay curled in a blue blanket in my mother's arms.

"What is it?" my father asked. "A boy or a . . ."

"A girl," Raheela Bibi said.

"A girl?"

"Yes." She looked at him. "A perfect, healthy baby girl."

"Can I hold her?" I scooped the blanketed baby out of my mother's arms. I traced a finger against her soft nose, her cheeks, and her curved chin, with a dimple like Safa's. Raheela Bibi was right; she was perfect.

My breath caught when she gripped my finger with her fist. She was so tiny, but her grip on me so tight, as though she knew I would always protect her. Any disappointment I might have felt at not having a baby brother dissipated like powder in a running stream.

"What should we name her?" I asked. "I have a notebook with the ones I like. Shifa is pretty, but I also like Maha. Maaria. Lubna."

That's when I realized the room was unusually quiet.

I looked at my mother. She was crying. I was so eager to see the baby, I hadn't noticed the tears streaming down her face. Until now.

My father stood by the door. His eyes were red.

"I'm sorry," my mother whispered.

"Nothing to be sorry about," he said. "God does what he wants."

Of course I had known they wanted a son. I heard the conversations of our neighbors and the whispers in our own house. But staring at my parents' expressions right now, I saw they didn't look disappointed; they looked crushed.

I hadn't been present when my other sisters had been born. Is this how they'd reacted then?

Was it the same when I was born, or was it okay since I was the first?

Sometimes I wish I did not pay such careful attention.

Maybe then I would not have learned that they thought being a girl was such a bad thing.

Chapter 6

Seema and I watched over our new sister in the living room while the morning sun filtered through the windows. We both had stayed home from school all week to help, but tomorrow was Monday, and I looked forward to going back. Our father had left for the fields after morning prayers, and Safa and Rabia were still asleep. I savored the silence, cuddling the sleeping baby in my arms.

"You see that?" I nudged Seema and nodded at the little one.

"What?" Seema yawned.

"She smiled in her sleep! She's going to be a happy one."

Seema patted the baby's soft, silky hair. "You think Amma is okay?" she asked.

"She's always tired after a baby is born," I said. I remembered how it was after Safa. Parvin made all our meals and put us to bed for at least a week.

"Not just that . . ." She fidgeted. "She was so sad."

"I know," I said. As much as I tried to block it out, my parents' expressions were etched into my mind.

A knock on the door interrupted our conversation.

"I bet it's Fozia Auntie." Seema stood up.

"Thought she'd have come before now," I said.

"Hope she brought jalebis." Seema said. Fozia was Hafsa's mother and usually the first to get details about any happenings in the village. No one could ever get too annoyed with her, though, because she usually came bearing her prize jalebis, the twisted, sticky orange treats that would lure anyone to the door. And with Hafsa's sister's recent engagement, she was making all sorts of desserts.

"Congratulations," she said when Seema opened the door. Fozia stepped into the house before pulling off her canary-colored chador and settling it around her shoulders. Hafsa tagged along beside her.

"There she is!" Fozia smiled at the baby and handed Seema her platter of assorted sweets before she walked over and took the little one from my arms.

"Didn't you say backaches meant boy, Amma?" Hafsa frowned.

"Yes. That's what my mother said, anyhow, but who can really predict these things? It's a shame, though. I thought for sure it would be a boy this time." Fozia clucked her tongue. "Is your mother handling it okay?"

I stared at Fozia. How could she hold my perfect little sister and shake her head with sympathy?

"Amma is sleeping," Seema said.

"Of course. Well, I'm on my way to the tailor. Hafsa's outgrowing her clothes every time I blink." She handed the baby back to me. "Tell your mother I came by?"

"See you at school tomorrow," Hafsa said, waving.

I shut the door.

"Did you hear her?" I fumed. "How dare she say that! Act so sorry for us—and with her own daughter standing right there!"

The tube lights above us flickered before shutting off. The overhead fans slowed to a halt. Another blackout. Seema rushed to open the windows. Last week's blackout left us without electricity for over two hours. Already I felt the heat rising from the concrete floor.

Rabia and Safa came running into the living room. Rabia's face was streaked with tears. She glowered at Safa. "She took my doll!" Rabia shrieked.

Before Seema or I could respond, Rabia took off after Safa, chasing her around the sofa. Safa laughed and skipped, tripping on the edge of our rug and skidding headfirst into the table. A glass perched on its edge trembled before crashing onto the floor. Water seeped onto her and into the rug. The noise echoed off the walls.

Now both girls were crying. My mother must have heard the commotion. She had to. I walked over to her bedroom and peeked inside. The curtains were tightly drawn. Her back was curled to the window, her eyes shut.

"Amma?" I asked softly, but she didn't respond.

The baby began whimpering in my arms. I took a deep breath, closed the door behind me, and looked at my sisters, both of their faces wet with tears. Amma never yelled at us. Despite the younger two and their constant arguments, she found a way to be patient. Until she was better, I had to try.

Fortunately, Parvin walked into the house just then. She carried a basket of laundry fresh from the clothesline and set it down before scooping the baby from me. "Let me get her to your mother," she said as the overhead fan whirled back on.

"She's sleeping," I said. "I just checked."

"Well, the baby needs to eat," she said. "Don't worry, I'll talk to her."

Seema soothed the girls while I cleaned up the shards of glass.

I hadn't understood how much my mother did to keep the house running until Seema and I tried to fill her shoes. Parvin helped us as always, doing laundry, washing dishes, and chopping vegetables for dinner, but the work kept piling up. And watching two boisterous little girls was a whole job unto itself. We were so busy, I barely noticed the call to evening prayers from the minaret in the distance or the sun setting outside our window.

Seema finished drying dishes with Parvin later that night while I put the girls to sleep. I was hoping to sit for a few minutes when I came out of their bedroom, but cringed when I saw the basket of clothing Parvin had brought in. My mother normally ironed all the clothes as soon as Parvin pulled them off the clothesline—it kept the cotton kamizes from getting hopelessly wrinkled—but today the clothes still sat in their basket untouched. Our school uniforms lay crumpled at the top of the heap.

"I'll get the ironing board," Seema said, reading my mind. "Let's at least get tomorrow's clothing sorted out."

I surveyed the house. The girls' dolls lay scattered by the sofa; the groceries Parvin picked up this afternoon rested in burlap sacks in the kitchen. Crumbs littered the rug. And there was still no sign of Amma being ready to get up and help. All she managed was to feed the baby. I still had to change the diapers.

"What's wrong?" Seema asked, returning from my parents' bedroom with the iron and narrow metal board.

"Everything," I said. "How are we going to keep up with it all and go to school? Look at all these clothes. It'll take me hours to go through them all."

"We'll figure out a system," Seema said. "You'll do the ironing at night after the girls go to bed, and in the mornings I'll get everything organized for dinner."

But I knew it was impossible. "I'm going to have to stay home," I told Seema.

"I'll stay home, too, then," Seema said.

"No. You just switched to the upper class a few weeks ago—you can't fall behind."

"But it's too much work for you to do alone."

"Parvin is here, too. We'll be fine. I'm sure it will just be a few more days until Amma's back to her old self."

I pressed the warm iron to Seema's uniform, hoping what I said was true.

Chapter 7

I prepared breakfast for my mother and stepped into her room. The sun was well into the sky, but the curtains were still drawn. The baby lay asleep next to her.

I had now missed nine days of school. My mother was still not better. She managed to come out of her room now and then to get a glass of water. Last night, she even sat listlessly with us in the courtyard for our evening meal. But she wasn't improving fast enough, and the longer I was away from school, the further I fell behind.

"I brought you breakfast," I told her. "I added onions to the omelet the way you like."

"Set it on the side table," she said.

"Amma, you need to eat to get your strength," I said.

"I think I need to rest even more."

I knew I should sit with my mother and encourage her to eat, but it wasn't as if she listened to me these days. I glanced at the window. Sunlight peeked from behind the curtains.

"I'm going to go to the market. We're out of ginger and peppers. Hafsa said they got a shipment of those biscuits you like. I could pick some up."

"No, thanks. But take Safa and Rabia with you."

"Parvin can watch them. It will take me twice as long if I take them."

"Your father doesn't like you going to the market by yourself."

It was no use protesting. Gripping Safa with one hand and Rabia with the other, I tried to measure my pace so they could keep up with me. The cool morning breeze and clouds thankfully shielded us from the otherwise oppressive heat.

The market was a ten-minute stroll, well past the tailor shop and the pharmacy, to the town that bordered our village. This was where nearly everything was, including the open-air market with all sorts of different stores and the vendors who sometimes showed up outside with carts of samosas and kulfis.

"What has the *S* sound?" I asked my sisters as we walked. "Who can find something with the *S* sound first?"

Safa craned her neck, studying the brick houses lining the road. Hira, the butcher's wife, waved to us from her front step as we walked past.

"Street!" Rabia pointed to the ground. "And stairs." She waved toward a neighbor's concrete steps.

"And Safa!" Safa grinned.

"Good job!" I patted their heads and picked another letter. This game I came up with was working! It kept them by my side. I thought I wanted to teach students closer to my own age, but I loved helping my sisters learn. Maybe I'd make a good primary teacher.

The open-air market came into view. We walked past Basit's butcher shop. He cleaned off a leg of lamb, readying it to hang on a ceiling hook along with the day's other fresh cuts of meat. The sweet maker next door studied his ledger next to the glass display of sweets in rows of orange, yellow, and pistachio green.

I could already hear the chatter of my neighbors before I stepped inside the produce store owned by Hafsa's family. It was the most popular store in the market. People even came from neighboring towns to buy from them because they had the best selection. I squeezed past a group of women examining the eggplants and made my way up to the blue crates filled with tomatoes, jalapeños, and radishes. My family's oranges and sugarcane were packed along the back wall. Not for the first time, I wondered how many other little stores all over Pakistan our produce might reach. I loved imagining all the far-flung people eating food that grew from the earth behind my house.

Grabbing what we needed at the market, I paid Hafsa's father, Shaukat, who seemed grateful I kept my hands so firmly on Safa this time. Last time, she knocked a stool into the wall, sending a shelf of spices crashing to the ground.

"The roof!" I looked up.

Shaukat looked at me.

"I thought something was different," I explained, pointing at the ceiling. "The blue tarp is gone. You fixed the hole."

"I did. Was hoping to make do longer with the tarp, but the wind last week tore it right off. Had to replace the whole roof."

"Well, it looks nice. And it's good it's fixed, isn't it?"

"It's never good to borrow from the Khan family." His jaw tightened as he rang up my order. "But sometimes you have to do things you don't want to."

Shaukat's words lingered in my mind as I left the market. Just like he didn't want to borrow money, I didn't want to leave my mother when she still hadn't recovered. But the longer I stayed home, the further I fell behind at school. I couldn't keep this up much longer. Amma needed help. We had to do something.

"Amal!" my classmate Farah's mother called out to me from a distance. She walked at a steady clip toward us.

"Mariam Auntie!" Rabia turned to me. "That starts with an *M*, right?"

"Good job!" I said. "Here." I dropped change into her palm. "Go get some kulfis from the man over there."

The girls hurried to the vendor as Mariam approached.

"Don't you look pretty in that shalwar kamiz," she said when she drew near. She reached out and smoothed the collar. "When I saw the floral pattern, I knew it would be perfect for you. Told your mother a little bit of lace would add some pop to it."

"Thank you for sewing it," I told her. "It fits me perfectly."

"How is your mother?"

"Tired, but she's doing okay."

"A girl, I heard?" She shook her head.

I knew everyone wanted to have a son, but I was getting tired of hearing this. Wasn't she once a little girl, too?

"Tell your mother I'll come this afternoon to check in on her. She must have some hand-me-downs she needs fixed up for the baby."

I thanked her before continuing on our way. I laughed when Safa smacked her lips on our way home. White syrup dripped down her chin onto her dress.

"You can't do anything without making extra work for me, can you?" I said.

I handed the groceries to Parvin when I got home and grabbed a towel to wipe Safa's face. My father sat at the table in the living room. He sorted through an assortment of papers scattered across the desk.

"Is everything okay?" I asked him. "You're home early."

"It will be," he sighed. "Work is busier than usual, and your mother's still in bed."

"We should phone Raheela Bibi. She'll know what to do."

"It's not something the midwife can cure."

"Then maybe we can take her to the doctor?"

"What she needs is time. She'll get better soon enough."

"But the thing is"—I fidgeted—"I've missed a lot of school now, and exams are coming soon. I was hoping I could go back to school tomorrow."

"Amal . . . Safa and Rabia need you."

"Parvin could watch the girls until we came back."

"Parvin has her own work to do, you know that. Your sisters aren't her responsibility."

"She won't mind! She loves the girls—"

"Enough, Amal!"

The sharpness of his voice silenced me.

"I'm sorry, Amal. But this is how it has to be now. You're the eldest daughter. Your place is here."

I wanted to tell him it wasn't my choice to be the eldest, but I held my tongue. Why did this random chance have to dictate so much of my destiny?

"In a week or so, we can see how things are going," my father continued. "But in any case, remember, you have already learned a lot. More than many of the neighborhood girls. You can read and write. What more do you need to know?"

I always thought my parents knew me well. So how could he ask me that?

What more did I need to know?

The whole world, Abu, the whole world.

Chapter 8

When I walked into the kitchen the next morning, Seema was ironing. "Why aren't you in your uniform?" I asked her. "You're going to be late for school."

"I'm staying."

"Seema."

"I got up early this morning to help with the laundry. You work the pile down and then it grows up again higher than before. The chores are endless. You need me."

"Parvin and I will handle it. You have to go to school."

"It's not fair." Seema's eyes grew moist. "How can I go when you can't?"

"It isn't fair—but you can't fall behind since you only just began. I want you to go."

Seema's eyes watered, but she slipped on her uniform. After she left, I watched her from the window. Hafsa would meet up with her a few steps out of my view. They'd enter the brick schoolhouse and settle into their desks and learn things I didn't know. I was the best student in my class, but soon Hafsa, and even Seema, would surpass me.

"The girls are still sleeping?" Parvin asked as she stepped inside and closed the back door behind her. I nodded.

"Good. We might actually get a head start on all the things we need to get done today. Omar will pick up cauliflower on his way home from school. We have enough potatoes, but I'll double check . . . What's wrong?"

Parvin came in and out, helping so quietly I could forget she was there, but it was Parvin who always double checked we had everything we needed to prepare our meals and keep the household running. She was the invisible arm propping the family up.

"Just . . . thank you," I told her. "We don't say it enough. Thank you for everything."

"What is this thank-you for?" she asked. "This is what family does. You'll get through this. Come here." She hugged me. "Everything will be fine."

I wasn't so sure about that, and I wasn't a little kid

like Rabia or Safa who was easily comforted by her hugs, but with Parvin's arms around me, everything did ache a little less.

"How was school?" I asked Seema when she came home that afternoon.

"It was good!" She smiled.

"Do you need me to look at your poem? It's due Monday, right?"

"Of course you have to look at it," she said. "But you have your own to write."

"Seema, Abu isn't going to budge."

"He doesn't need to."

"What do you mean?"

She stuck a hand in her book bag and handed me a folder.

"What's this?" I asked her.

"Take a look."

I parted the folder. The poetry assignment. The spelling test. The math test.

"But, Seema, I can't write a poem without a lesson on it. And how can I take the tests—"

"I'll test you," she said. "I talked to Miss Sadia, and she agreed: As long as you keep up with your work and take the tests, she'll keep you on the roster. I also promised her I'd take good notes and teach you the lessons myself. Even the poetry lesson. Don't look at me like that! I can do it! And I'll teach you everything I learn. Because you *are* coming back." She gripped my shoulder.

I read Miss Sadia's familiar scrawl on the first paper.

> *Hi, Amal—This is a lot, I know. But if anyone can do it, you can! I'm rooting for you.*

I hugged Seema. I thought hope had vanished. But hope was a tricky thing. It found its way back to me.

Chapter 9

The girls were busy watching television and Seema and I were getting settled at the table to go over her notes for the day's geography lesson when my mother's friends knocked at the door.

"I come bearing laddus this time," Fozia said, stepping inside with Mariam. "Is your mother up for visitors now?"

"She's still not feeling well."

"Now, this is too much! She has to start meeting people eventually," Fozia said.

Fozia was right. Something had to be done to snap her out of her fog. Maybe visitors would help.

I stepped inside my mother's room.

"Amma," I said, "Fozia and Mariam Auntie are here to see you and the baby."

"This isn't a good time." Her voice was dull. Even though the room was dim, I could still make out the circles under her eyes etched so deep, I wondered if time would ever erase them.

Lubna lay swaddled tightly, fast asleep. It's what I was calling the new baby, though it wasn't officially her name. My mother didn't name us until we were a year old and she knew for sure we would survive. I picked her up and cradled her in my arms.

"They only want to say hello. I'll straighten up the room a little and tell them to come in."

"I'm sorry." She reached out and stroked my arm. "I'm foggy lately. I'll shake it off soon."

"I know you will," I managed to say.

Her gold bangles from her wedding dowry, the ones she never removed because they were her most valuable possessions, clinked against her arms when she touched me. Her frame seemed smaller than it did a few weeks earlier.

I drew open the curtains and put away the handful of clothes scattered on the floor.

"You can come in now," I told her friends.

• • •

I took my time making chai and arranging a plate of biscuits on a wooden tray. By the time I carried the tray into my parents' bedroom, I was surprised to see my mother sitting up and chatting.

"It's devastating," Fozia was saying. "I've been there myself, you know."

"I'm not sure how one even recovers. Or if you even can," my mother responded.

I stared at my mother. It was one thing to feel this way when my baby sister was born, but to still think it now?

"Munira can't possibly recover. He burned their orange groves to a charred crisp," Fozia continued.

"I heard it was her children playing with matches in the field," Mariam said.

"Yes, of course you heard that—who would dare accuse him openly? Mark my words, one day he's going to hurt the wrong person," Fozia said. "These things catch up with you."

"He runs this town. Men like him suffer no consequences," my mother said.

My hands unclenched. It was the Khan family they were talking about.

"Never thought I'd say this, but it was better when his father was running this town," Fozia said. "Sure, Khan Sahib threatened all sorts of things, but did he ever do them? To teach a lesson here and there, yes. But his son Jawad? Ever since he took charge, things are out of control. I really think he enjoys punishing people."

"Owe him nothing, and he cannot harm you," my mother replied.

"Except everyone does," Mariam said. "We need his filthy money. Maybe if we all united against him, something could be done. It's happening more and more these days—people are banding together and overthrowing their landlords. Read about it in the newspaper all the time."

"The Khan family would never let that happen here. Remember Hazarabad?" Fozia asked. "The people in that town made a pact. Refused to pay their debts until he stopped with the threats. Forget Munira's measly acres! He destroyed their entire village. Every last orange grove and cotton field. Jawad Sahib sent quite the message!"

My mother lifted the teacup from the ground and brought it to her lips. She took a sip. "I'm thankful we're on the other end of the village, far away from him," she said.

I gathered their empty teacups. I didn't really care about Jawad Sahib and his acts of vengeance. My mother could have been discussing the devil himself for all it mattered. I was just glad to see my mother drink her tea. It had to be a sign.

I stepped into the kitchen as my father came home. He slipped off his shoes on the woven mat by the front door.

"Fozia and Mariam Auntie are in with Amma right now," I told him excitedly. "She's drinking chai and talking. She even smiled."

"Good!" my father said. "Maybe she's starting to get better."

Why didn't I push her to meet her friends sooner? I went into my bedroom and ran my hand over my uniform hanging in the closet. It was starched and ready. Maybe in a few days I could wear it again.

"Amal," my father said. He watched me from the doorway. "I didn't mean to get your hopes up. Drinking a cup of tea is nice, but it's still going to take time for her to fully recover and be up and running the house again."

"But maybe—"

"No, Amal. I'm sorry, but it has to be this way."

But did it really have to be this way? If I were a boy, would I be staying home to fold laundry and iron clothes? If I were a son, would he so casually tell me to forget my dreams?

I rushed outside and sank onto the front steps. My mother was adamant about our education. If only she could get better, everything could go back to normal.

"Look who it is!"

Hafsa pedaled up to me on her younger brother's bicycle. She dug her sandals into the ground, slowing it to a halt.

"Do your parents know you're riding a bicycle again?" I asked her. Most people around here frowned upon girls riding bicycles, and Hafsa's parents had let her know they were one of them.

"If my brothers can ride a bike, then I can, too," she said. "Besides, maybe I'll be the next Zenith Irfan and bike across the country."

"That was a motorcycle," I reminded her.

"Same difference."

The voices of children playing cricket in a nearby open field floated over to us.

"How's Seema as a teacher?" she asked.

"The power's gone straight to her head." I let out a small laugh. "She won't even repeat the questions on the spelling test, no matter how much I beg."

"Sounds like Seema." Hafsa smiled.

"How's Miss Sadia?" I asked. "Ever get her that bell?"

"Ha. I wish. She asks about you every single day, though." Hafsa rolled her eyes. "If we thought you were her favorite before, we definitely know now."

"Well, you can become her new favorite." I swallowed. "My father doesn't seem like he'll be letting me go back to school anytime soon."

"No way! You better be back. We're going to go to college, remember? I'm not rooming with a total stranger."

"Let's hope he changes his mind, then."

"Hope?" Hafsa's frowned. "You think my dad doesn't grumble about all the money my books and uniforms cost him? But he knows it's less of a headache to send me to school than to keep me home. You can't just hope, Amal! You have to keep at him, and don't take no for an answer."

After Hafsa left, I thought about what she had said. Maybe she was right. I had to come up with some kind of plan—but I also knew no plan could work if my mother wasn't better.

Chapter 10

The lights flickered off again the next afternoon. The overhead fan slowed to a halt. Another blackout. My forehead trickled with sweat.

Seema was back from school and doing her best to corral Safa and Rabia, whose shouts echoed off the concrete floor, hammering into my brain.

It turned out my father was right about yesterday. The cup of tea with Fozia and Mariam wasn't any sort of magic cure. As usual, my mother spent the morning with the curtains drawn. She barely spoke a word when I went inside to check on her.

She wasn't on the mend.

Maybe she never would be.

I had to get out for a little while.

I counted the money I needed for the market.

Seema's back was turned to me.

"Get your hands out the flour!" she yelled at a powder-white Safa.

I'll get her, I wanted to say, but the words never left my mouth.

I was allowed a few moments of peace without any of my sisters yanking at my sleeve, wasn't I? Just this once?

I slipped past Seema and out the house.

It was only a trip to the market, but I would cherish this time to myself.

The sounds of tractors, bicycle bells, and children playing cricket in the street filled me with a sense of calm.

I knew each store owner and vendor I passed. I knew their wives and their children. But today, traveling the same streets I'd walked hundreds of times before, without little hands to keep out of fruit stands, without tiny feet to steer around idling rickshaws, I noticed it all as though for the first time. The sun was hotter than usual for the time of year, but I even enjoyed this.

Shaukat's store was bustling. My neighbors filled the aisles, sifting through the vegetables and fruit.

"Why is it so busy today?" I asked my neighbor Balkis.

"New arrivals. Pomegranates. Coconuts. Apples," she replied. She waved at the shoppers with one hand and fanned her face with a newspaper with the other. "Needed some turmeric but didn't know I'd have to fight these crowds. You'd think Shaukat was giving things away for free."

I squeezed through the aisle. Two pomegranates rested in the crate perched next to the onions and apples. Red, sweet, delicious pomegranates. I counted my money. I had enough to buy one extra item. Something small. Just for me.

I snatched one up as a woman grabbed the other.

One of my neighbors argued with Shaukat over bruised zucchini and squash. I grabbed a handful of onions and some ginger and leaned past her to pay.

Slinging my satchel over my shoulder, I stepped back onto the dusty road. I gripped the red fruit in my palm. Maybe this pomegranate was the sign of hope I needed. A bit of sweetness after all the bitterness. I would share it with Omar and Seema. It didn't make everything better, but the thought made me happy.

Even now, I can remember how happy I felt in that moment.

That moment before my world changed.

One second I was standing.

The next, slammed backward onto the ground.

A car. Black with darkened windows. How did I miss it? How wrapped up in my mind was I not to notice a car?

The door opened and footsteps approached.

I took in the clean-shaven face, the closely trimmed hair, and the eyes hidden by dark sunglasses.

People began to gather by the side of the road. Balkis, Hira, Shaukat, customers from the market. Why didn't any of them help me? Why did they stare at this strange man and say nothing?

I stumbled to my feet. My hands were scraped and bloody. My leg throbbed when I put my weight on it, but I could stand. I gritted my teeth and gathered the bruised ginger and onions lying scattered along the road and tossed them in my satchel.

"You should pay better attention," the stranger said. I saw his hand reach down and pick up my pomegranate.

He stepped closer to me. "Are you hurt?" he asked. "Where do you live? I'll take you home."

He was smiling. His teeth were so white, the whitest I had ever seen.

"I'm fine," I told him.

I reached up to adjust my chador, cloaking myself from him. I was about to walk away when I realized he was still holding my pomegranate.

He followed my gaze.

"My mother loves these," he said. "You won't mind if I take this for her, will you? Of course I'll pay you for it and you can buy more."

"It was the last one."

"Will this do?" He pulled out a handful of money.

What was he doing?

Did he think I was a beggar?

That everything was for sale?

My mother's voice told me to let this go. Something was off with this man. Let him have the fruit and walk away. But all I could see was the red pomegranate and how he grasped it in his palm as though it was already his.

I thought of my father, who had no time for my dreams. My little sisters and their endless demands. Suddenly I felt tired. Tired of feeling powerless. Tired of denying my own needs because someone else needed something more. Including this man. This stranger. Buying me off. Denying me this smallest of pleasures.

"It's not for sale."

"So you'll give it without charge?"

His smirk taunted me. My scraped hands burned.

"You hit me with your car and want to take my things?" My voice trembled; I heard it growing louder, as if it were coming from someone else. "I'm not giving it away." I snatched it from his hand.

The crowd murmured. I started walking away.

"Stop!"

His voice was so loud, it echoed off the buildings.

I didn't stop.

I walked quickly until I turned the corner toward home. Only then did I break into a run.

The farther I ran, the sicker I felt.

Who was that man?

What exactly had I done?

Chapter 11

The knock on the door the next morning sent my heart racing. I opened it slowly, half expecting to see the man with the dark sunglasses, but it was Fozia. She came empty-handed today. I waited for her to ask me about yesterday—if there was gossip, Fozia would have been one of the first to hear it—but she barely glanced at me before going to see my mother.

I lingered by my parents' door while my mother and Fozia talked about the baby. As they discussed what to do about Lubna's sniffling, I stood there and waited for the words to leave Fozia's mouth. To tell my mother what happened.

Finally, Fozia said, "I'll pick up the baby's medicine for

you. I was on my way to the market anyway. Glad you're doing better."

She stood up. She walked past me, and I watched her leave.

Why didn't she say anything? Maybe I made a bigger deal out of what happened.

Either way, I learned my lesson. I would follow the rules from now on. I would never step so much as a toe out of this house without one of my sisters with me.

"Read to us?" Rabia asked me that afternoon. She brought a book and pulled on my arm.

I had spent the day working as hard as I could. I mopped the floors and scrubbed the walls. I folded and put away all the laundry and chopped up the onions for dinner.

I sat down on the sofa with her and Safa. I smiled at the story she chose. My father had bought it years ago for me when he went to Lahore.

"You know this was my book once?" I asked.

"We know," Rabia said. "That's why we love it!"

I read them the story about a kitten who decided to adopt a basket of mice. I laughed along with my sisters when the kitten scolded the mice before they scattered, running in every direction.

I was so engrossed, I didn't hear the door swing open and Seema charge in until she grabbed me by the arm and ushered me into the kitchen.

"They're talking about it," she said before I could say a word.

"Who is?"

"Everyone! They're talking about yesterday."

Before I could ask her more, the door opened again. My father.

"Tell me it's not true." Sweat trickled down his forehead. "If you tell me it's a lie, I will believe you."

"I'm sorry," I whispered.

"Amal." His hands fell to his sides. "Talking back to Jawad Sahib, of all people . . . What have you done?"

Jawad Sahib?

My mouth went dry like the dusty earth.

Fozia called him worse than his notorious father.

And I yelled at him. In front of everyone.

"He wants a word with me. This Friday. One of his officers dropped off this note." He held up a crumpled piece of paper. "Didn't know what was going on until the workers told me."

"A-Abu," I stammered, "I should have told you right away. But his car. It hit me. I was minding my own business walking home from the market. But he wouldn't let me be. He wanted to give me a ride home. He took my things and wouldn't give them back!"

"I don't care if he wanted your entire satchel of things!" my father snapped. "You give it to him. You drop everything at his feet, apologize, and walk away! Don't you have any idea the lengths that family goes to just to satisfy their egos? And Jawad Sahib especially! Don't you know what he could do to us now?"

"Malik, enough. You're scaring the little ones."

It took me a second to recognize my mother out of bed. She stood at the archway of her bedroom door, the baby in her arms.

"Do you have any idea what your daughter's been up to?" he shouted.

"I didn't know who he was," I whimpered.

"Did it matter? Have we not taught you how to act in public? Bite your tongue one minute and prevent a lifetime of burden."

"And yelling won't solve this," my mother said. "Let's talk again once we've calmed down."

"It's not fair." Tears slipped down my cheeks. "His car hit me. He took my things. Why am I the one in trouble?"

"Since when has life been fair?" He shook his head.

"You can read books and tell me the capital of China, but you have no idea how the world works. God only knows how he will find it fit to punish us."

"He wouldn't do anything serious over something so small, would he?" I asked.

"He's done far more for far less."

All this over a simple pomegranate, still lying uneaten in my satchel buried beneath my bed. I thought of the person from the car, the gleaming white teeth, the close-cropped hair, and the way his voice went from sweet like honey to cold and dark within seconds.

I thought of the stories I'd heard all my life, the way Shaukat's jaw clenched at the mention of his name. The way Fozia said he loved to dole out punishments and had personally burned an entire village to the ground.

So what kind of punishment would he dream up for me?

Chapter 12

I got out of bed as the sun peeked its head over the horizon. I hadn't slept in two days. Jawad Sahib would be here tomorrow.

Stepping into the kitchen, I blinked: My mother was out of bed again. She perched on a stool on the ground, kneading dough for buttery breakfast parathas like she used to. Her waist-length hair fell unbraided in waves around her shoulders.

"You're up early," she said. Her eyes were red. Her cheeks blotchy.

"I'm sorry," I said. Guilt pooled inside me, liquid and dense.

She wiped her floured hands with a rag and stood up.

"I'm the one who should apologize," she told me. "I haven't been a good mother lately."

"No, Amma, please don't say that."

"You're my eldest, but you're still a child," she said to me. "I don't know—it's like I'd fallen into some kind of well the last month. Everything was so dark. It happens for a while each time I have a child."

"Because we're girls," I whispered.

"What? That's not true." She gripped my hand in hers.

"I was there. You were crying. You wanted a son."

"Yes, we did want a son," she sighed. "But it doesn't mean we don't love our daughters. You're part of me; how can I not love you?"

"Why is having a boy all anyone can talk about?"

"Who else will care for us in our old age? Who will run the farm and keep your grandfather's dream alive?"

"I could," I told her. "Seema and I both would."

"You will get married one day. Then you'll belong to a new family."

"But I'm part of *this* family!"

"I wish it wasn't this way, but this is how the world works. It doesn't mean I don't love my daughters. I love each and every one of you."

"What are we going to do, Amma?" I whispered. "I made such a huge mistake."

"Don't you worry. We'll fix it. We will."

I used to sit with my mother most mornings as she made breakfast in the early hours while everyone slept—it was the only chance I ever had to be alone with her. I would tell her what I learned in school, the latest drama I might have had with my friends. If anyone could come up with a way to fix this, she could. She always knew how to make things right.

When Omar and Seema returned from school, we gathered by the wire chicken coop in the backyard, obscured from view.

"I've been running it over and over in my head," I told them. "I still can't figure out what he's going to do tomorrow."

"He's not going to do anything," Seema said. "If he wanted to do something, he'd have done it by now. Everyone knows he doesn't think—he acts."

"The things he's done, though . . ."

"Rumors," she said. "They're just rumors."

I looked at Omar, but he twisted the heel of his sandal in the dirt. He didn't meet my eyes.

I didn't want to tell Seema about Munira's blackened fields. I couldn't bring myself to correct her.

Afraid if I said it out loud, it might come true.

"Don't worry." She put her arm around me. "By this time tomorrow, this will all be behind us."

Chapter 13

The hard-knuckled knock on our front door sent a chill through our household early the next morning.

Seema and I sat up in bed. Safa and Rabia had slept with us last night. Safa began to speak but, upon seeing our faces, stayed silent.

The front door creaked open. Footsteps echoed through the house.

I pressed my ear against the bedroom door.

"Welcome to our home. It's an honor," my father said. "I'll call my wife to prepare tea."

"I'm not here for tea. I'm here about your daughter." That voice, the same cold voice from the day at the market. His voice was ice water poured down my spine.

"Sahib, we are beside ourselves over what happened. Please. Forgive her foolish mistake."

"Forgive? How can I forgive when the harm is done? I take some of the blame for this disrespect. I haven't been as involved with matters around here as I used to be. People forget what they don't see."

"We haven't forgotten. We are forever in your debt."

"Yes," he replied. "You are. And given the circumstances, I'm left with no choice but to collect."

Collect? What was he talking about?

"Please, Sahib. I have no means to pay you back yet. You know how little we have."

No. This couldn't be right. It was the one thing our mother always said: Never take on more than you could bear. And never be indebted to anyone—especially someone like this.

"If I had the money, I would lay it at your feet, but I don't have it."

"Then she will do."

There was a long silence.

"I don't understand," my father finally said.

"She will live on my estate and work for me. She will pay off your debts."

"She—she's practically a child," my father stammered.

"I would like to let it go, but if I let this pass, who will disrespect me next?"

"Sending my daughter away like this. I can't, Sahib."

"She will be treated like all my servants, no better, no worse. I'll even let her visit twice a year like the others."

I backed away from the door. I heard wrong. I must have. But why, then, did Seema stare at me like she saw a jinn? She motioned me back to the door.

"I'll give you a few days to discuss, but I promise you will like the alternatives far less."

The door opened and shut. A car engine sprang to life. Tires rumbled against dirt and gravel.

The room was shrinking.

Closing in on me.

Flinging open the kitchen door, I rushed into the backyard, past the workers in the sugarcane fields, past the tractors, their noise blurring into the distance.

"Amal! Wait!" Seema raced after me.

But I didn't stop. I kept running, as if the farther I went, the farther I could leave my destiny behind.

Chapter 14

"Over my dead body." My mother's voice was low, almost a growl.

My sisters and I lingered by the closed entrance of my parents' bedroom. It had now been two days since Jawad Sahib visited our home and my parents began arguing without end.

"You discuss this as though there's a choice," my father said. "Is our daughter not dear to me also? Be reasonable."

"So we give up our respect? She goes off to become a servant, and what becomes of her? And what about the rest of our girls? They are young, but think of their futures. Who will marry a girl whose family has been shamed like this?"

"I spoke with the village elders. Our neighbors feel

sympathy, not judgment, toward us. This won't change anything for the other girls. Besides, it could have been worse. It's not as if she'll be out in the fields. She'll be a servant in that house. And Jawad Sahib gave me his word; he won't harm Amal."

"His word? His word can change with the tides. What need does he have to keep his promises? You're the one who took loans from a viper without breathing a word to me. You fix it."

"Do you hear yourself? When the rains came five years ago and destroyed all the wheat before we could harvest it, or when the drought shriveled the sugarcane to dust last year, how do you think we survived? A miracle? I did what I had to do to protect this family."

"I would rather have died than owe him a thing. And thanks to you, we owe him our daughter."

"Who doesn't owe him money? Make the monthly payments and there's no problem. None of this would have happened if you hadn't decided to stop functioning. Children were running this home. What else could we expect?"

There was a long silence. Then my mother wept.

I walked away from the door and into my bedroom. I wished Seema was home from school. My stomach hurt more and more these days. My guilt was hollowing me from the inside out.

The door creaked open. In a place so filled with people, spaces seldom stayed empty for long. But it wasn't one of my little sisters who walked inside. It was my father.

He sat next to me on my bed, his eyes fixed on his sandals.

He had avoided me since we last talked, but sitting next to me now, his eyes damp, his shoulders hunched, he didn't look angry. He looked like my father.

"I shouldn't have taken money from him," he said. "I was desperate. He preys on people in their moments of weakness. I thought I'd pay it back with the next harvest, but the debt kept growing. I owed money on what I owed. He told me I could take my time. I thought he was generous. Now I know the truth. How else to keep us forever under their thumb?" His eyes locked into mine. "Do you know how hard your grandfather worked to buy this little patch of land?"

"I know," I whispered.

"When I was your age, we went hungry for months, saving everything we could. My father wanted us to be our own masters. To have something to pass down to future generations. I'm the only son in my family; it's up to me to keep this land ours and honor your grandfather's memory. Does everything our family worked for come to an end now? This isn't what any of us want."

"Abu, I can't leave. What if I never come back?" I pushed down a sob.

"Never come back?" He placed his arm around me. "You think I'd let you go away forever? He wants his money. I'll get him his money. I swear on my life I will get you home as soon as I possibly can. I'll make things right."

"How long?" I wiped a tear. "How long will I live there?"

"A few weeks. A month at the most. You won't be there long."

I looked at the pile of books in the corner of my room. A month ago, I washed the chalkboard with Miss Sadia. I sat with Omar on the fallen tree. I was going to be a teacher.

How could everything as solid as the earth my grand-father fought for crumble so easily beneath my feet?

Chapter 15

Jawad Sahib's driver would be here any minute.

My suitcase was packed and resting by my bed. My mother had lent me the aluminum-cased one from her own wedding dowry. She filled it to the brim with clothing, nuts, and dried fruits.

There was a tap on my bedroom door, and then Hafsa entered. She closed the door and approached me. "I was thinking about it last night," she whispered. "What if you ran away? Maybe hid in my house?"

"Hafsa, I couldn't do that."

"My parents wouldn't even need to know," she said. "My closet is pretty big. Nobody would ever guess you were at my place and it could give us some time to figure out what to do next."

"I can't. It wouldn't be safe, not for me and definitely not for you," I told her.

"But that's what friends do." Hafsa's eyes watered. "You would do the same for me."

"I know." I gave her a hug. "It means a lot, but if I don't go, he'll go after my family."

And besides, I thought, how long could we keep it up, anyway? It's not as if I could simply run away without looking back. This was all I knew. My roots sank too deep into this earth.

When we stepped out of the bedroom, Fozia was sitting with my mother on our sofa. They wore cotton shalwar kamizes, white, the kind some wore when attending a burial.

"I knew he was wicked." Fozia's eyes welled. "But who knew he was the devil himself?"

"Did you pack everything you need?" Seema asked me.

"I think so. Don't know how I managed to squeeze it all in."

"Room for one more?" She handed me the doll from my childhood, the one our mother made for each of us.

"You found it?" I scooped up the soft, worn doll and pressed its fabric against my nose.

"I decided to think like Safa. I found it wedged between the bundles of old clothes in the closet."

"Thanks, Seema." I hugged her. Our damp cheeks pressed together. I didn't know how I could handle this if Seema wasn't here. She would help Rabia and Safa through this. She would watch over our family.

"Everyone keeps crying." Rabia tugged at my leg.

My sisters hadn't left my side all morning. The little ones clutched my kamiz.

"It's time, isn't it?" Parvin said, as she and Omar joined us.

Parvin's expression was drawn. I wanted to tell her how much I'd miss her, but the words lodged in my throat. Instead, I hugged her.

I longed to hug Omar too, but in such a crowded room I didn't dare.

"I should have come up with a solution," he told me. "I was up all night. Nothing. I couldn't think of anything."

"Abu promised he'll get the money," I said. "I shouldn't be gone long. A month at the most." I tried not to focus on the fact that he wasn't here. He had stood over my bed early this morning watching me while he thought I was asleep. He had kissed my forehead. I realized now, he was saying goodbye.

A car pulled up outside. The engine cut off.

I glanced around my home, taking in one last long

look at the worn sofa and handmade rug. My family and friends.

Rabia and Safa were still attached to me. I lifted them up one at a time and pressed my face to their soft cheeks. I kissed them twice, then three times, but would I ever get enough?

There was a knock on the door.

My mother pressed a clump of money into the palm of my hand, along with a gray phone. "It's Fozia's old phone. Call as soon as you can. Let me know you're safe." She wiped my eyes. "You will be strong. You will hold your head up high. No matter what happens, no matter where you are, you're my daughter."

I kissed Lubna. I hugged my mother one last time. I had hardly ever stepped outside my home without someone by my side. Now I was leaving alone.

A gray-haired man in an ill-fitting suit was at the door. He picked up my suitcase, and before I lost my nerve, before I ran away and never stopped, I followed him toward the waiting black vehicle. I opened the door and sat inside.

So many firsts.

My first time in a car.

My first time feeling cool air pressing against my face.

My first time saying goodbye to everything I had ever known.

Chapter 16

The familiar stretches of brown and green patchwork earth I had known all my life swept past me in a blur before transforming into plush manicured green as the car slowed down and the driver turned onto a gravel road lined with shade trees.

When the estate materialized in the distance, only the second-story windows and balconies were visible from behind the huge brick wall surrounding it.

An armed guard with a grim expression let us in at the wrought-iron gate. The steel lock clicked loudly when the gate shut behind us.

The driver walked me into the cavernous house and

dumped my things next to a marble staircase in the middle of the foyer before turning to leave.

"Wait, Ghulam. What's this?" asked a gangly teenager with a mop of curls. He stared at me from across the foyer.

"How should I know?" the man grumbled. "I'm Nasreen's driver, not his. Why I'm stuck running his errands is beyond me." He walked away, his footsteps echoing into the distance.

The teenager stood in a sunken living room with over-sized sofas. Next to him stood a younger girl, about my age, with a sharp jaw and straight brown hair. Floor-to-ceiling windows behind them overlooked a tiled verandah with wicker sofas and a sprawling garden.

"I think that's the new girl Mumtaz told us about," the girl said. "Remember?"

"What do we need a new servant for?"

"How should I know, Bilal?" She turned to me and asked, "Do you know where you're supposed to go?"

I shook my head.

"Where's Mumtaz?" the girl asked Bilal. "She'll know."

"Probably in the servants' quarters."

"Can you take her?"

"Nabila, you know I have to get these shoes to Jawad Sahib. I'm already running late."

"Well, if she stands there gawking, it'll be us he yells at

for not putting her to work." She sighed and walked over to me.

"Come on," she told me. "Let's find Mumtaz. She'll know what to do."

"Well, good luck." Bilal nodded to us before he hurried away.

I lugged my suitcase and tried to keep up with her, but it was hard not to get distracted. This house was unlike anything I'd ever seen. Back home I could touch my ceiling with my hand if I stood on a chair, but here the ceilings seemed to graze the sky. Grim-faced family members stared at me from photographs lining the egg-white hallways. Each room we passed was larger than the one before it, and all were filled with brilliant rugs covering marble floors. Light poured in through enormous windows.

I followed Nabila through a curved entrance down a new hallway. Everything was darker and shabbier here. Instead of marble floors, this part of the house had gray concrete. The cooled air of the main home was replaced here by hot musty air and the smell of frying onions.

A man in a faded shalwar kamiz holding a broom and a dustpan brushed past me as he headed toward the main house. A woman followed behind carrying a basket of laundry—pants and shirts and shalwar kamizes piled in a heap.

"Your arm any better?" the woman paused to ask Nabila.

"Oh." Nabila glanced down. Only now did I realize her left arm had white gauze wrapped around it. "The burn looked worse than it was. The tray was too bulky and there were too may things on it."

"Well, keep it bandaged for a week," she said. "Make sure it doesn't get worse."

"I will," Nabila said to the woman. "Did you find out how long Jawad Sahib's going out of town for?"

"I know he's leaving after dinner. Bilal just loaded a pretty big suitcase into his trunk. It's got to be at least a week or two, but hopefully longer." She smiled before continuing on.

Nabila ushered me farther down the narrow hallway and stopped at a rickety door. It creaked when she pushed it open.

"This is the only spare room, so it must be yours," she told me. "You're next to Shagufta, the woman I was just talking to."

I took in the cramped, windowless space, empty except for the worn charpai. This wasn't a bedroom. It was a prison cell. Beads of sweat prickled my forehead.

"What's going on?" a voice said.

It was an older woman with a nose ring, like my mother's.

"This is Mumtaz," Nabila told me before turning to her.

"I was looking for you. The new girl arrived"—she gestured toward me—"I didn't know where to put her."

"She's going to be in the room next to Nasreen's."

"Nasreen Baji's room?" Nabila stared at her.

"I know. She just told me," Mumtaz replied.

"But why?" Nabila asked.

"How should I know?" Mumtaz glanced at my suitcase. "Bring that along with you into the kitchen for now. Nasreen wants you to get acquainted there. She'll meet with you after dinner."

I lifted my suitcase and pushed back my growing dread.

"It's hard at first, I know," Mumtaz said gently. "But you get used to it."

Get used to it?

I thought of Safa and Rabia shrieking through the house, Lubna sleeping in my arms, the sound of Omar's bicycle chime.

That was the life I was used to—and it felt as distant to this one as the stars in the night sky. The stars that could no longer guide me home.

Chapter 17

I trailed Mumtaz into a kitchen that featured a metal sink the size of a table. Fluorescent lights hung over counters that ran the length of the room. The windows against the far wall were cranked open, but the slight breeze did nothing to cool the hot, stuffy room. Just outside the window was a simpler verandah for the servants, with some threadbare charpais and stools stacked against a wall.

A girl who couldn't have been more than nine years old chopped onions but paused to smile at me. Next to her, a man with a gray mustache stirred three different pots.

"The dishes," Mumtaz said, and pointed to a towering stack in the sink. "Start on those."

I rested my suitcase by the door and walked to the sink.

Pressing down the faucet, cool water rushed against my hands, a welcome reprieve from the stifling heat.

"Officers gone?" the cook asked.

"Left a little while ago," Mumtaz said.

"I hate serving him food after they leave," he grumbled. "He finds something wrong with everything after they come."

"I know. They have really been putting him on edge lately," Mumtaz said.

"His father shouldn't have given him so much responsibility if he's going to be so thin-skinned."

"If you think you have it bad, Hamid, think of Bilal," Mumtaz said. "Poor guy is with Jawad most of the day and has the bruises on his arms to prove it. Be glad you're mostly out of sight back here in the kitchen."

"Never thought I'd say it, but I miss his father," the cook said.

Mumtaz plucked cream-colored ceramic bowls and plates with gold trim out of the cupboards while the little girl ladled cholay, beef korma, and saffron-scented rice into serving platters.

"Can I help?" I asked when I had finished the dishes.

Mumtaz nodded to a pile of kebabs resting on a plate by the stove. "Get the kebabs from Hamid and put them out on one of the flat trays."

I arranged the kebabs on a platter and sprinkled them with chopped cilantro like I did at home.

Mumtaz picked up a serving bowl and gestured for me to pick up the platter. "Come along," she said.

After the gossip and banging of pots in the kitchen, the main house was eerily silent.

"At last she arrives," Jawad said when I entered the formal dining room and placed my platter on the sideboard next to Mumtaz's tray. He had no sunglasses on now, and his eyes bored into mine. I quickly looked away.

His servant, Bilal, stood against the wall. He watched me curiously.

"Enjoying it here so far?" Jawad Sahib continued.

I couldn't move, rooted by his gaze. *Breathe*, I reminded myself. I would not let him see me cower.

"Not scaring the girl on her first day, are you?" said a woman as she entered the room. She wore a silk shalwar kamiz, her graying hair swept up into a bun. Jawad Sahib leaned up and kissed her on the cheek.

"You should thank her." He nodded to the woman. "My mother was in the car that day you ran into us. She's the only reason you are here at all. I had other ideas on how to handle your disrespect."

His phone vibrated against the table, and his attention shifted.

"Go." He waved his hand at me and picked up the phone.

I hurried toward the kitchen. My mother always said the best way to feel better was to do something, anything. And she was right; making myself useful had always helped.

Nabila was lifting an iron pot from the stove and maneuvering it toward the sink. I moved to help her, but before I could offer, the pot slipped from her hands and crashed to the concrete floor. The noise pierced my ears. Bits of leftover food splattered onto the ground and the adjacent wall.

I grabbed a rag from the counter and leaned down to wipe up the mess.

"Stop," Nabila said.

"It looks worse than it is," I told her. "We can clean it up in a minute."

"I took care of myself before you came and I'll take care of myself when you're washed out and long gone."

"Nabila," Mumtaz chided.

The rag hung limp in my hand as I stared as Nabila. She lifted the pot and rested it in the sink. How did I make an enemy within an hour of arriving?

The kitchen began to fill up as other servants filed in for their lunch. I recognized some of them, like Shagufta, who had been holding the laundry when I entered the servants' quarters earlier, and Ghulam, the driver who brought me here. I picked up a porcelain plate, but then I noticed the others grabbing metal ones from a separate cabinet. Their drinkware, too, came from the separate cupboard.

I put the porcelain plate back down. I couldn't explain why it bothered me so much. It wasn't as if I ever ate out of anything much fancier than what was set aside for us here, but Parvin and Omar ate out of the same plates and drank from the same cups as we did. There was a clear dividing line here, and I had to understand where I stood. We could prepare the platters and wash the porcelain plates and glasses, but we could not eat from them.

The young girl came over and held out an empty plate for me.

"I'm Fatima. What's your name?" she asked.

"My name is Amal." I took the plate from her.

"Do you live here now?" she asked.

"I guess. I mean, for a little while I do."

"My father made this food. He's a really good cook. Khan Sahib pays him extra so he won't go anywhere else. The korma is one of his specialties."

"I love korma." I said. I ladled some onto my plate. The roti was cold but I didn't mind, as I was nearly dizzy from hunger.

"His nihari is even better. He makes it for breakfast

sometimes. I can get you some lemons for it when he makes it next. I know where he keeps them."

"Fatima, come eat before everything gets even colder," her father called to her.

I followed Fatima to the entrance of a room attached to the kitchen. The servants sat cross-legged in a circle on the floor. Fatima sat down next to her father. The plates rested on their laps.

"Is it true?" asked the servant who had been carrying a broom earlier in the day. "She hardly seems the type to do such a thing."

"She's here, isn't she?" Ghulam said between mouthfuls. "Kids these days like to mouth off—don't care much for respect."

"He let her off easy," Nabila said, looking at me. "If the rumors are true, he could have done worse."

I walked back into the kitchen and rested my plate on the counter. I understood people talked about other people—I was guilty of it myself—but how could they say such things when I was right there?

That's when I saw Jawad Sahib. He watched me from the kitchen entrance.

"I had one question for you." Jawad Sahib smiled. "Was it worth it? The pomegranate you couldn't bear to part with?"

I'd promised myself I wouldn't cry in front of him, but my body betrayed me. Hot salty tears slipped down my face. I looked down and stood still. I did my best not to move.

I stood still until he was satisfied. Until he walked away.

Chapter 18

After dinner, Mumtaz led me up the marble staircase onto a carpeted landing. The second floor was as big as the first floor. Nasreen Baji's room was the first one on the right just off the landing. Stepping inside, I saw a white bedroom set with cream sheets. A matching white armoire and dresser were in the distance. A makeup table rested next to a closed bathroom door. Light glowed from beneath its slats.

I followed Mumtaz into an attached room that turned out to be an enormous closet filled with Nasreen Baji's clothes and shoes. Through the closet we entered another room, rectangular and compact. The walls were a pale blue, with a border of elephants and giraffes.

"This is where you'll be staying," Mumtaz said.

"Here?" I looked around at the nursery. "This is my room?"

"There are many who would do a lot for a room in this part of the house. Now, put away your things, and then meet Nasreen," she said before leaving.

I thought of the stuffy, windowless concrete room from earlier today. Mumtaz was right. This room had air-conditioning and a blue tiled bathroom with a porcelain sink and chrome handles like I'd seen on television. I unpacked my suitcase and glanced at the door, wondering what lay in store for me on the other side.

The light still glowed from beneath the closed bathroom door when I stepped back into her room. I glanced at my satchel. I'd forgotten to put it away, but I did need to call my mother just to let her know I was safe. I took out my phone, but a knock on the bedroom door made me jump. Jawad Sahib stepped inside.

"Bored already?" he said, looking at my phone.

Is this how it would be here? This man lurking around every bend and curve?

"I wanted to let my mother know I'm all right."

"Your obligations are to me now." He grabbed the phone from me. "The more you learn how to leave your backward ways behind, the easier things will be for you. Your days of being an idle farm girl are over."

Idle farm girl? Backward ways?

I stared at my phone in his hands. My mother would tell me to be quiet right now and ignore these words. But how could he tear me from my home, take away the only connection I had to it, and then pronounce me backward? The words couldn't be stopped.

"I've never been idle. I went to school. I cared for my sisters. I helped my family." My voice broke. "The ones you took me away from."

He looked at me as though watching a field mouse develop the skill of speech. His eyes narrowed.

The bathroom door opened.

"Jawad, what's going on?"

"I'm telling her how things will be."

"That's my job, isn't it?" She walked up to him. "If you take that away, what is there for me to do?"

"You're right." He kissed her cheek. His anger from moments earlier vanished.

They chatted a bit longer. He told her he was heading out now. Bilal was staying back this time. He asked her to keep an eye on him. He told her he would stop by her favorite sweet shop on his way home. He promised to call.

And then, he tucked my phone into his pocket and walked away, taking the one lifeline I had to my family with him.

Nasreen Baji walked to her makeup table and sat down on the cushioned bench. I watched her, uncertain what to do. Did I ask her how I could help? Or wait for her to tell me what she needed? Was I supposed to stand with my hands to the side? Or folded in front?

The list of things I didn't know was endless. I stood frozen by the door.

Nasreen Baji tapped her fingers against the table and then glanced into the mirror.

"I could use some help," she told me, and when I walked up to her, she nodded at the brush on the table.

I picked up the wooden brush and parted Nasreen Baji's hair. I'd done this for my mother and sisters countless times but never performed such an intimate task on a stranger. Nasreen Baji's hair was straight and brown with threads of gray. My mother's hair was black like the night sky, falling over her shoulders in waves. Last time I brushed my mother's hair, taking care to gently tease out the knots with my fingers, she hummed lullabies to Safa, who lay curled in her lap.

Thinking of my mother kept my hands steady.

"Did Mumtaz tell you what you are expected to do in this household?" she asked.

"No," I told her.

"You are here for me and anything I may need. You bring my meals and wait on me. When there's company, you wait on all of us. You massage my head if it hurts and bring me my migraine medication. You will sleep with your door open so if I need you, you can hear me. Understood?"

I nodded.

Before she could say more, the phone resting on the makeup table vibrated.

"My husband." She picked up the phone.

Khan Sahib.

I was so afraid of Jawad Sahib, I'd forgotten about his father, the monster in my childhood dreams. The bogeyman our mothers used to threaten us with when we were slow to finish our meals. He slept in this very room.

"Thought you forgot to phone me," she said when she answered. "Gazala called this morning. She switched her dinner party to next month for us. I told her we'll be there." She listened and smiled. "Yes, glad something can wrench you from politics." They spoke a little longer before she hung up.

"He's away more than he's here. Off with my eldest boys in Islamabad. Chasing politics at his age. Can you imagine?"

I tried to mask my relief. At least there was that—the man who haunted my childhood dreams was hardly ever here.

"You must be missing your family," she said. "This can't be easy."

Unlike her son's, her words contained no malice. I nodded.

"I can relate. Of course I married into the family, but no matter the circumstances, missing your family feels the same. You're from Nabay Chak, aren't you?"

"Yes."

"I'm from Banway Chak."

"Banway? But that's a ten-minute walk from my house! It's on the other side of the market."

"True," she said. "You know the Marali family?"

I nodded. The Marali family was a huge clan, scattered over many of the nearby villages.

"That's my family."

Now that she mentioned it, I could see the family resemblance in her straight dark hair and her high cheekbones.

"Najam and Sana were my classmates," I told her.

"My sister's children." Her eyes brightened. "How are they?"

"They were doing well last time I saw them," I said. "I've known them since I was five."

"Smart girls. Khan Sahib will pay for college when the time comes. I'll make sure he does. Tell me. Is Masud Baba still running the produce store at the market? He was my father's closest friend."

"Shaukat, his son, runs it now."

"Shaukat?" Her expression fell. "Well, that's a shame."

"He does a good job," I said. "His prices are fair, and he sells the best produce."

"Yes, I'm sure," she said. "It's just I knew him when we were little. He had different dreams back then."

I tried picturing Shaukat as a child sharing his dreams with the woman in emerald earrings sitting across from me. I couldn't.

"But . . . how did you end up *here*?"

Nasreen Baji began laughing.

I stiffened. Why did I say that aloud?

"Blurting things out used to get me in trouble, too, when I was your age," she said. "Just be careful. My son didn't inherit my sense of humor.

"Our marriage surprised many people," she continued. "Khan Sahib's family is distantly related to the Maralis. He saw me at a family wedding. His parents wanted a bride from a wealthy family, of course, but when you're the youngest, you get your way."

Nasreen Baji told me about her family back in her village, and it turned out we had other neighbors in common. She was so easy to talk to, and the more she spoke, the less intimidating she seemed.

It was the strangest thing to find within these walls someone who was more like myself than I could have imagined.

For the first time since I arrived, I felt a little less afraid.

Chapter 19

My first job the next morning was to get Nasreen Baji's breakfast tray ready to bring up to her. The meal was a simple one: tea, toast with a dollop of jam, and a plate of sliced apples. Mumtaz showed me where the trays and teacups were kept in the kitchen before she left to sweep the terrace. I turned on the chai percolator and arranged the tray. Nabila wiped down the countertop next to the sink. Fatima swept up crumbs from the floor while her father stored chopped vegetables in the refrigerator.

As I waited for the water to heat, I looked out the window. With Jawad Sahib gone, the servants were relaxed and our verandah was busy. Toqir, the elderly servant who dusted and swept the main level of the estate, rested on a charpai.

Shagufta sat on a bench and chatted with another cleaning girl. The gardener was still holding a clipper in one hand as he was drinking tea and chatting with a few other men.

When the chai was ready, I poured it into a porcelain cup etched with hummingbirds. Fatima tugged at my kamiz. "You want to try some?"

"Try what?" I asked.

"The chai," Fatima said. "I can get you a cup from the other cupboard."

"I don't think I'm allowed."

"If they don't find out, then it's not wrong. That's what Nabila always says. She sneaks things all the time!"

"Hush!" Nabila glowered at the girl.

Fatima reddened and hurried to the back of the kitchen.

"She's just a kid," I told Nabila. "She didn't mean anything by it."

"You don't get to come here for a day and tell me what she did or didn't mean."

I wanted to ask her what her problem was, but I bit my tongue. She could hate me for whatever reason she wanted, I thought. My father was collecting money for me at this very moment, and soon enough, I'd be gone.

Mumtaz hadn't mentioned how much sugar Nasreen Baji took, so to be safe, I placed five sugar cubes in a crystal bowl and set it on the tray.

"What are you doing?" Nabila frowned at my tray. "Why aren't you using the proper breakfast tray?"

"Proper breakfast tray? I got this one from the drawer Mumtaz showed me."

"There's more than one drawer." She smirked and pointed to a cabinet under the sink. "She uses the pink one with the gold trim for breakfast. Always has."

I walked over to the sink and leaned down to open the cupboard and sift through the fancy plates and serving dishes. I craned my neck. There were no trays. Would Nasreen Baji be angry if I served her breakfast on the wrong one?

When I walked back to the counter, the tray I'd prepared was missing.

"She took it." Fatima sat cross-legged, peeling potatoes. "She took it," she repeated. "Probably went to Nasreen Baji herself."

I rushed down the hall and up the stairs into Nasreen Baji's bedroom. Nabila stood in front of Nasreen Baji holding the tray in her hands.

"I'm sorry." Nabila's voice shook. "I wanted to make sure you had it exactly the way you liked it."

"But you're not my maidservant anymore, Nabila. You understand that, don't you?"

She looked down at the ground and nodded.

"Go on now and check with Mumtaz to see what needs to be done in the kitchen."

Nabila set down the tray on the nightstand by the bed and rushed past me. Her elbow bumped sharply into me. I walked over to Nasreen Baji and mixed in her sugar—two cubes, she told me. Like my mother.

"I'll make it with the right amount of sugar next time." I handed her the cup. "And I'm sorry about the tray. I should have paid better attention."

"Nabila is having a difficult time adjusting to the new situation." Nasreen Baji took a sip of tea. "She was my maidservant before you came."

"She was? But why did you replace her with me?" I blurted out.

"Nabila is a good girl, but she just made too many mistakes. The timing of your arrival was perfect. I was planning to replace her anyway."

I carried the tray back down the stairs to the kitchen and thought about Nabila. It was clear she despised me almost since the moment I arrived. But it made sense now. My life had changed overnight—and hers had, too.

Chapter 20

"Some of us are trying to work. You might want to try it," Nabila said to me later that week as I made my way down the stairs carrying Nasreen Baji's empty breakfast tray. Nabila was dusting the chandelier with a long brush and shot me one of her hateful glances as I passed.

I could have stated the obvious—I was working, wasn't I? But what was the point? It looked like I had an enemy whether I liked it or not.

I rinsed out the teacups and glanced out the window. A breeze swept through the trees. A handful of servants rested on charpais. Maybe I could get a chance today to step outside for a little while and feel the fresh air against my face.

Fatima poked her head into the kitchen. "Nasreen Baji wants to see you right away."

I dried my hands against a towel and hurried upstairs. Nasreen Baji was about to shower when I left. What could have happened?

When I stepped inside, Nasreen Baji stared at her armoire. She wore a teal-blue robe. Her lips were pressed together into a thin line.

"Amal, what did you do?" She pulled out a silk shalwar kamiz from the armoire. I gasped. The kamiz was charred straight through the center. I had ironed it along with three other outfits yesterday. I took care to use the gentlest setting. It took nearly an hour to press out all the wrinkles.

"Burning this is bad enough," she said. "But to hide it from me? As if I wouldn't notice?"

"Burn it? But, Nasreen Baji—"

"I shouldn't have assumed you knew how to handle expensive fabrics like these. You're not to touch my things again until Mumtaz goes over all the settings with you. Understood?"

But I knew how to iron. Just because we were not as rich as she was didn't mean I had never handled nice things. But I saw her expression. She'd already made up her mind. She wouldn't believe me.

"I'm sorry," I mumbled before leaving the room.

When I walked into the kitchen, Nabila was there.

"Too bad about the ironing," she said.

"What? I didn't . . ." My voice trailed off.

"I'd be careful," she said, brushing past me. "Nasreen Baji does not tolerate mistakes very well."

I stared at her retreating figure. Nabila did this! But what could I do? It was my word against hers. Why would Nasreen Baji believe me when she barely knew me?

I rushed outside to the servants' verandah and inhaled a deep breath to steady myself. Whether in the sugarcane fields or by the leafy stream bordering my family's land, being outside had always calmed me.

But it was different here.

Looking out at the perfectly trimmed lawn only made me miss the dirt backyard of my parents' home. And no matter how beautiful the fragrant gardens were, they were surrounded, as I was, by ten-foot brick walls.

I was outside, but the walls reminded me that I was not free.

"Malik's daughter, aren't you?"

I recognized the man addressing me as Ghulam, the driver who had brought me here. He was with Bilal, Jawad Sahib's gangly servant. They sat on low-seated woven stools, a brass hookah between them.

"I worked for your grandfather when I was a child," Ghulam said. "Chopped the sugarcane and helped harvest the wheat. Recognized your house as soon as I pulled up."

"Her family owns land?" Bilal asked. He cocked his head up and scrutinized me.

"I'd say a good twenty-four acres at least." The older man nodded.

"Ah. So even the mighty can fall down, too." Bilal laughed.

How easy it was for Bilal to laugh. His laugh was a pinprick: not sharp enough to cut, but deep enough to sting. I had Nabila to set me in my place. I didn't need more.

I turned to walk back into the house.

"Oh, come on. I didn't mean to upset you." Bilal said. "We're not so bad, I promise."

"You don't have to make fun of me! I'm just trying my best to fit in."

"Looking like you'll shrivel into dust at a few words isn't fitting in. It's only going to make things worse for you," Bilal said. "We heard what happened today. What are you going to do?"

"Nothing." I folded my arms. "I'm not going to sink to her level."

"That isn't fitting in," Bilal replied. "That's letting people take advantage of you. Talk back and hold your own. Or lose it forever."

"I don't need it forever!" I said. "And back home—"

"Except you're not back home, you're here," the older man interrupted. His voice was neither harsh nor mocking. Instead it was filled with pity. "Pay attention. Learn. You decide how you will be treated."

I walked back into the main house.

They were right.

My father would come and take me home any day now, but until then I had to play by the rules of this house. And that meant I had to stand up for myself.

Chapter 21

"Let the kitchen staff know they don't need to bother with my lunch," Nasreen Baji said the next morning. "I won't be back until dinnertime."

"Yes, Baji," I said. "And Mumtaz said she'll show me the settings for the iron today."

"Oh, that." Nasreen looked up at me and sighed. "I meant to talk to you. I know you didn't do it."

"You do?" Relief flooded my body.

"I have my eyes and ears in the household," she said. "The person responsible has been handled."

"Thank you, Baji."

"Good choice on the flowers, by the way." She nodded to the crystal vases on the coffee table and the nightstand.

I had replaced the drooping violets this morning with white and pink roses.

"My mother loves roses. We had them all around the border of our house."

"What colors did she have?"

"Only red," I told her. "I didn't know you could grow so many different kinds."

"My father had a plot of land for me to garden in when I was young, in the back of our house. I tried all sorts of flowers. Tulips, marigolds. Somehow I managed to always kill them. Vegetables were another story, though; I had a knack for that." Her eyes seemed to look past me when she spoke.

"My mother loves to garden, too . . ." I told her, my voice trailing off. Was my mother pruning her garden right now? Was Seema helping her instead of me?

"It was the funniest thing," she said. "I could be upset about anything at all, but digging through the garden, I found peace."

"What do you grow in your garden here?" I asked her.

"Here?" She laughed. "Imagine that! What would people think? The matron of the estate crouching in the back garden, planting mint?"

Maybe she was right, but then what was the benefit of

reaching Nasreen Baji's station? If she could be this wealthy and have power over so many people but couldn't grow her own garden, what kind of freedom was that?

After Nasreen Baji left and I finished straightening her room, I went to find Mumtaz. A bedroom door farther down the hallway was wide open when I passed. Bilal and Nabila were inside straightening it up. I took in the bed with navy linens. The furniture inside was the color of crushed almonds. Jawad Sahib's room. Nabila looked up. I was about to avert my eyes, but I remembered Ghulam and Bilal's advice. I met her eyes with my own steady gaze. I thought she would say something, but instead, she frowned and looked away.

I hurried down the steps to the main floor.

Mumtaz wasn't in the kitchen.

I walked past the dining room and then down a dim hallway with cream carpet I had not entered before. The first room I passed was a bathroom with black counters.

I paused at the next door. It was encased with six square windows. Peering through the glass, I saw a table with a leather chair beside a large window. A row of silver filing cabinets lined the wall behind it. But the other walls were lined with bookshelves that stretched from floor to ceiling. And books—so many books, they seemed to burst from the shelves.

A library! I couldn't believe my eyes.

I slipped inside, walked up to a shelf, and traced my fingers along the spines.

Poetry, fiction, history, biographies, the library had them all. Mirza Ghalib, and Allama Iqbal, Miss Sadia's favorite poet. I had never seen so many books in one place before.

And then I saw it. On the bottom shelf. A collection of poetry by Hafiz. I remembered the book Omar lent me by the stream. The poetry unit Miss Sadia was so excited about. I pulled out the title. It was a thinner volume than Omar's, and the cover was green, not orange.

I looked at the book in my hand. I knew I shouldn't have touched it. I shouldn't have even stepped inside this room. But if I borrowed one thin volume, returning it as soon as I finished, would anyone notice? Was it really a crime to borrow a book gathering dust? Wasn't it a bigger crime to have such an amazing library collection going unread?

I tucked the book under my arm, obscured by my shawl, and hurried to my room. For the first time since I came here, I felt happy. I wished I could tell Miss Sadia and Omar that I'd found a way to read poetry after all.

Chapter 22

"Any word on Roshanara?" Nabila asked Mumtaz as we worked together in the kitchen. They diced onions and tomatoes, piling them into a metal bowl. Bilal lingered by the counter. I stirred the chai pot for Nasreen Baji and her guest, who were on the main verandah.

"She's visiting her mother," Mumtaz replied.

"She left over two weeks ago."

"Roshanara's not coming back," Bilal interrupted. "He told her not to."

"What?" Nabila's knife clattered to the counter. "He fired her?"

"Jawad Sahib said her work wasn't up to his standards."

"But she needed this job," Mumtaz said. "She's the only one working in her family."

"Like he cared," Bilal said.

It was hard to follow their gossip. I was counting down until the day I could put this place behind me and pretend it was just a bad dream. No matter how much the job paid, why would anyone choose to be here?

A tap on my waist. Fatima held up a blue package of cookies.

"These are the ones she likes to serve guests," she told me. "Can I help you with it?"

I set the cream plate with scalloped edges on the table. Fatima opened the bag, pulling out the square shortbread cookies.

"Have you ever tried the chocolate ones?" She pointed to the pantry by the window.

"I haven't," I said. "Are they good?"

"The best!" Her eyes lit up. "She puts them out when her older sons visit because they love chocolate. They're a little expensive, so we can't eat too many or they'll notice. But I can get you one if you want."

"Maybe another time." I smiled. "But thanks for the tip."

"Fatima, go get me more onions," Nabila interrupted us.

Fatima set down another biscuit.

"Now," Nabila snapped.

I picked up the last biscuit, pressing it with my finger until it snapped.

"Whoops," I said. "It broke. Want it?"

Fatima grabbed both pieces from me, stuffing them in her mouth.

I returned Nabila's glare with a smile and carried the tray outside.

Pouring the chai into each cup, I served Nasreen Baji and her guest, and then stood in the back against the wall as I always did during her visits. The conversations she had with her friends weren't much different from the sort my mother had with hers, except in addition to the usual gossip, they discussed potential brides for Jawad Sahib. Today the women were sifting through photos of possible matches. I felt sorry for any girl who would have to put up with a man like him.

My mind wandered to the last book I had borrowed. I hoped I could find the time to return it sometime today and get a new one. I glanced at the clock. It was a little past noon. Rabia and Safa were likely dressing up their dolls or jumping rope in the courtyard right now. Omar and Seema were in school. My father would be tending to the farm. Was my mother better? Was Lubna laughing yet?

"The literacy center is coming along nicely," her guest

said, tucking the photographs back in her purse. She wore a maroon shalwar kamiz and matching lipstick.

"Yes." Nasreen Baji nodded. "It should be open in another month."

"Everyone is talking about it. It's the first time the organization broke ground in Punjab."

"Adult literacy centers are the new thing these days," Nasreen Baji said. "My husband thinks his support of this one will help win him the election."

"Anyone sign up yet?"

"No one," Nasreen sighed.

"Who turns down a free education?" The woman shook her head. "They enjoy being illiterate is the problem, really."

I thought of my classroom, thirty-four girls crammed two to a desk. I could still remember how the heat rose from the ground and pressed into our skin during the warmer months and how we shivered under our chadors and sweaters when the temperature dropped. Even so, we went to school every single day we could. Nasreen Baji knew better. She had to know better. She had to tell this woman she was wrong.

But Nasreen Baji didn't say a word in protest. Instead, she asked me to bring them more tea.

"She looks like a good one." The visitor nodded to me

as I gathered their plates and cups onto the tray. "You must tell me where you get them."

I balanced the tray in my hands and walked to the kitchen. I tried to pretend I didn't care what the woman said, but I did.

I doubted I would ever get used to being discussed like cattle at the market.

Chapter 23

Later that week, I ran Nasreen Baji's bath and sprinkled lavender petals into the water. I laid out her clothes on her bed as she stepped into the bathroom.

I glanced at the clock. I had ten minutes.

Slipping into my room, I grabbed the book hidden beneath my pillow. I tucked it under my shawl before heading downstairs to return it.

After finishing a few poetry books earlier in the week, I had read my first biography. The story of Allama Iqbal. Omar would have laughed at me for picking up such a heavy tome, but choosing thick books meant I could hold on to them longer before I needed to exchange them. And now I understood why Iqbal was Miss Sadia's favorite poet. It turned out he wasn't just a poet. He was also a politician, a teacher, a lawyer, a scholar, and a knight. I thought one dream was enough for a person, but reading his story, I learned some people could hold on to many different dreams and see them all come true.

I went down the hallway leading to the library, past Toqir, the elderly servant who dusted the baseboards. He didn't even glance at me as I passed him. Slipping inside, I put the book back into its spot and ran my hands over the other titles. I paused at the thick black dictionary on the bottom shelf. Omar always wanted one of his own; he said dictionaries contained every word ever uttered. I pulled it out. It was heavier than expected. The paper was thinner than in the other books, and the font was tiny. I smiled. What if I read this whole thing? What would Omar say when I told him I read all the words to ever exist?

I heard footsteps. Toqir. I tightened my grip on the dust rag, my ready excuse for why I was here. But before I could slip the dictionary back onto the shelf, I saw it wasn't Toqir. It was Jawad Sahib. He stood at the entrance, blocking me.

"And what do you think you're doing here?" he asked.

"I'm dusting." I gestured to the dust rag and tried to keep my voice from trembling.

"And that's why you're holding my book?" His eyes narrowed. "I thought you'd have learned your lesson by now, but I return home and learn my new servant has been stealing books from me? I have to say that takes a great deal of nerve."

"Stealing?" I gasped. "Never!"

"I bet you saw my books and thought they'd fetch a big price, right? But you could sell a thousand of them and never make enough to pay off what you owe."

"I would never steal from you, Sahib. I borrowed some books, yes. But I returned all of them."

"And who said you could walk in here and take my things?"

My face flushed. He was right.

"I shouldn't have," I said. "And I'm sorry. But these books . . . You have so many. There's dust gathering on their spines. I couldn't help it. Forgive me, I've missed reading so much."

There was a long pause.

"You can read?" he asked.

"Yes. Of course."

"Can you write as well?"

I didn't know whether to be offended at his presumptions or relieved the storm clouds seemed to be parting, revealing blue skies and sunlight.

"I can write. I can read. I know math as well."

He studied me for a moment.

"Full of surprises, aren't you?"

But his words weren't filled with his usual contempt.

"I can't remember the last time I read one of these books," he said as he walked to the bookshelf and examined the titles. "I might have been your age when I read *A Stranger in Al-Andalus*." He pulled the book from the shelf. "I loved this one. Read it so many times, my father replaced my worn copy with a new one. He didn't realize I liked the feel of the old one."

I tried imagining him as a teenager, sentimental about a worn book. I couldn't.

His mobile phone rang. He glanced at the phone and then at me.

"I'm letting this pass," he said. "See? I can be a forgiving man, but don't touch my books again."

He lifted the phone to his ear and motioned for me to leave.

I stepped into the hallway. He let me go. He didn't punish me.

Nothing happened. Everything was fine.

I should have felt grateful.

But the thing was—those books were what made my days bearable. They were what helped me sleep at night without my homesickness choking me.

Without books, what was there to look forward to?

Chapter 24

Nasreen Baji had a migraine headache. I had spent half the night massaging her head, but it hadn't helped, and now she grimaced over lunch.

"I can draw your bath when you're finished," I offered. "The steam helps sometimes."

"Rest will do more good." She clasped a hand to her forehead and stood up. "Mumtaz is gone for the afternoon to visit her sister. Keep an eye on the kitchen until she returns."

"And tell Bilal I'll be in the library catching up on some work," Jawad Sahib told me. "He shouldn't bother me unless I call for him."

"What kind of work?" Nasreen Baji asked.

"Just some accounting and paperwork."

"But why? Zaid should be doing that. What do we have an accountant for?"

"Whether or not he is an accountant is debatable, and the only one I can trust is myself anyway," he said. Then he looked at me. "How are things going with her?" He nodded toward me.

"Very well," Nasreen Baji said. "She is a gift from God."

"Good. I'm glad it all worked out," Jawad replied.

I'd settled dirty dishes into the sink and had just turned on the faucet when I felt a tug on my kamiz. Fatima looked at me. Her expression was somber.

"What's wrong?" I turned off the water.

"I heard about what happened yesterday. About the books."

I flushed. Toqir must have told everyone all about it.

"So you know how to read?" she asked.

"Yes. I learned at school."

"Could you teach me?"

I paused at the unexpected question.

"Baba said he could get me paper and pencil."

I glanced at Hamid. He covered a pot with a metal lid and rested his cooking spoon to the side. He gave a small nod.

"But I might not be able to learn," she continued. "My mother used to say I wasn't very bright."

She said it without any affect, as though it was simply fact.

I picked up a butter knife and held it out to her.

"What is this?" I asked her.

"A knife."

"What kind of shape does it have?"

"Long. Straight?"

"That's the first letter in the alphabet. Alif."

"Alif," she said slowly.

"See?" I said. "You're learning to read already. I can teach you whenever we have time. It's not so hard, I promise."

Her eyes widened. She took the butter knife from me and rushed off to show the cook.

I finished the dishes and wandered out onto our verandah. With Jawad Sahib back, it was empty. Fatima's words kept coming back to me. Why would any mother say something so cruel?

Something moved in the distance. I squinted. It was a cat. Orange and white. I walked over to where it was stretched out under the sun.

"Peaceful out here, isn't it?"

Nabila stepped outside and joined me in the garden bordering our verandah. She set down a metal bowl filled with milk on the grass. The cat walked over to Nabila, brushed herself against her, and purred.

"She's a stray." Nabila petted the cat. "She wandered over my first week here. Been giving her milk ever since. I named her Chotu."

"She's pretty," I said tentatively.

"She is," Nabila said. "When I first came here, I sat by those flowers any chance I got." She pointed to a flush of purple in the distance. "I don't know their names, but they grew next to my parents' house. I would look at them, really fixate on them, and for a little while I could pretend I was home."

"When did you come here?" I asked her. These were the first words she'd spoken to me not laced with malice.

"I was nine years old," she said. "As old as Fatima is now."

"To pay back debts?"

"There were no debts until they brought me here." Her expression darkened. "I was traded in for the price of six goats and a cow for my eldest sister's wedding. My parents promised they'd come back to get me as soon as they repaid him."

"They didn't come?"

"They came, all right. Borrowed more money. Maybe they could have paid it all back, but then there was the money we owed for living here."

"What do we owe for living here?"

"Don't you know? Nothing is free. Not the stale rotis, the bed we sleep in. Not for you and me, anyway. It's different for Mumtaz, Hamid, Toqir, and some of the others. They choose to work here. They get paid for the work they do and can live here or with their families. You and me? We aren't free. We work off our debts by working here, but the food we eat, the sheets on our bed, and the roof over our head are all accounted for and piling upon the original debt."

"But that makes no sense. If he charges us to live here, how can we ever pay it off?"

"We can't."

I thought of my father. He promised to bring me home as soon as he paid back the debts, but how could he pay back Jawad Sahib if every minute I spent here made the balance higher than the day before?

I sank onto a bench and tried to steady my breathing.

Nabila was wrong. She had to be.

But if she wasn't, did this mean I would never be free?

My chest burned with the unjustness of it all. Until that moment I didn't know heartbreak was a real and physical breaking.

"It gets easier with time," she said. "Look at me. Look at Fatima."

"Fatima has her father," I said.

"Hamid isn't her father."

"What?" I looked at her. "What happened to her? Why is she here?"

"The youngest of seven girls is what happened to her," Nabila said. "Dumped her here when she was six years old. Still remember the day," Nabila said. "She curled up in a corner of the servants' quarters. I think Hamid must have looked like her father, because out of all of us, she went running straight into his arms and clutched him tight. Called him Baba. Never saw him crack any real emotion until then. He's watched over her like she's his own since then."

It wasn't fair, I wanted to say.

But didn't my father always say life wasn't fair?

Now I understood just how right he was.

Chapter 25

I stepped into the garden as the sun was rising. Flecks of pink and violet streaked across the sky. I'd spent another night pressing Nasreen Baji's head. She was finally asleep when I slipped out, the dark eye mask covering her face. My own eyes burned from exhaustion. Nabila's words kept playing in a loop in my mind since yesterday.

A gray sparrow landed steps from my feet. Safa used to chase any bird that dared to land near our house. Omar teased her with a reward if she ever caught one. Until now, I didn't realize how memories clumped together. Remembering one unlocked another and then another until you were drowning in a tidal wave threatening to sweep you away.

I thought as time passed my memories would hurt less, but grief was a funny thing. One minute I thought I'd made my peace, and the next I remembered my house so clearly I could almost touch it.

The longing threatened to claw my insides raw.

Tears slipped down my cheek.

Why did I do it? Why did I let my temper get the better of me that day outside the market? Regret, I was learning, was the sharpest knife there was.

The sparrow pecked the ground a moment longer before she fluttered her wings and flew above the tree line, over the brick walls, and out of sight.

I felt someone else's presence. Looking back, I tensed. It was Nabila.

"It's hard, but it gets easier with time," she said.

"That's impossible." I said.

"What I do is keep my family, my friends, my old life, all in a separate part of my heart and try not to go there too often. The more parts you keep closed, the less it can hurt you."

But I couldn't forget my family and friends. It did hurt to think about them, but I was not going to forget them just because I was bound to this estate. If I stopped remembering my life before this, what reason would I have to go on?

"It helps to look forward to things," she said. "I'm visiting my family in a few months. I'll get to see my brothers and sisters. My cousins, too."

She smiled. It was the first time she smiled at me. Without the harshness of her downturned lips, she was beautiful. Maybe Mumtaz's words had settled in. Maybe she finally understood my circumstances were the same as hers. Whatever the reason, I appreciated the truce.

"I also like spending time in the garden," she continued. "I look forward to feeding Chotu every day. It's not much, but having things to be happy about, even little things, helps. Sometimes I go to the marketplace down the street from here. They have all kinds of things there—even books sometimes."

"There's a market?" I asked her.

"Yes, just about a five-minute walk from here," she said. "I don't have any money to buy anything, but I like browsing the snack stall and looking at the different fabrics for sale."

"We can go to the market all by ourselves?"

"If we finish our work and no one needs us, why not?"

I looked at the brick walls surrounding the property. Who knew when I'd have enough free time to actually see the market for myself, but the thought of walking past the gates and being away from this house—even for just a few hours—eased a little of the ache settling into my chest.

Chapter 26

"How's your headache, Nasreen Baji?" I asked her the next morning.

"Thanks to you spending the last two nights massaging my head, much better. I'm heading out to meet a friend for a little while."

"I'm glad. What should I do while you're gone?"

"You deserve some rest." She finished applying her lipstick. "Just finish tidying up the room and you can have the rest of the time to yourself until I return."

I thought it would be days, weeks maybe, until I could venture beyond this estate. My head was foggy from another sleepless night, but when would I have this chance again? I quickly straightened her room after she left and slipped on my satchel.

"Where are you off to?" Mumtaz asked when she found me in the foyer.

"Just a walk. Nasreen Baji said I could have the afternoon to myself while she was gone."

I hurried down the foyer and out the door.

Sliding my shawl over my head to shield my eyes from the bright sun, I approached the gate and the stocky guard holding a rifle. I had forgotten about him. I edged closer to explain myself, but before I could even say a word, he wordlessly swung the gate open. All this time I thought he was here to trap me inside, but it was I who had decided I could not leave.

I walked until the lush grounds of the estate melted into the main road. For a brief second I considered turning right, toward home. But it took so long to drive here. I could never walk home and back in one afternoon.

I craned my neck. A smattering of buildings dotted the horizon. I followed a few winding roads until I reached the market. I paused. From a distance it had looked like my own open-air market. There were even signs for the butcher, sweet maker, and milk store. But the buildings were boarded up. There was no one here.

The sun blazed down as a wave of heaviness settled over me. Even if the market had been a perfectly fine one, it wouldn't have been *my* market. It wouldn't have been Shaukat selling fruit. There would be no Seema. No Hafsa. No Safa.

I walked past a block of brown and gray slab homes. No children played outside. No women sifted lentils or dusted rugs. A faded newspaper lay crumpled next to a front stoop. I edged over and read the date. It was two years old.

I remembered the rumors about Hazarabad, the village Fozia had said Jawad Sahib had personally destroyed. I hadn't fully believed them. Until now.

I tried to hurry back the way I came, but the road I took ended at a blackened field. Skeletal orange groves filled the landscape.

By the time I found my way out of the maze of streets and alleyways, perspiration soaked my clothing and tears blurred my eyes.

It was the strangest thing to see the Khan estate and feel relief.

Stepping into the foyer, I felt the welcome blast of cooled air. Then I heard Jawad yelling. His voice echoed down the hallway.

This was the first time I'd ever heard him yell. His quiet penetrating glare was intimidating enough, which is why hearing his voice echo off the marble now made me cringe. Poor Bilal. Working for such a man couldn't be easy.

Then I heard a high-pitched sound, like an injured kitten. Inching closer, I saw Nabila. She was in the dining room, and Jawad Sahib towered over her.

"You helped her run away."

Run away?

"I had nothing to do with it. I swear!"

Jawad Sahib lifted his hand.

He was going to hit her. He was going to hit her because of me.

"Wait," I cried out. "Don't!"

Jawad Sahib's eyes widened when he saw me.

"Where were you?" He walked toward me.

"The market," I managed to say. "I got lost coming back."

"What market? There is no market. You dare lie to my face?" he shouted.

"I know that now." I trembled. "I came back as soon as I could. I wasn't running away."

"Are you a guest in my home?"

His voice vibrated through my body as the realization dawned on me—Nabila had played me again. She spun me a tale, and I believed every word. I needed to explain to him exactly what happened this time.

But before I could respond, Jawad Sahib did.

Until that moment, I never knew a slap had a taste.

A metallic taste in your mouth, like blood.

Someone gripped my elbow. They pulled me toward them. Nasreen Baji.

"Jawad!"

"I'm not letting this go unaddressed."

"It's addressed. You've made your point. Don't lay another hand on her."

"She was running away!"

"Running away? What is she doing here, then?"

He leaned toward me.

"Changing your mind doesn't buy you penance. I'll decide your punishment, but you will never disrespect me again."

He walked away without another word.

Didn't he understand?

Wasn't this—my being here—punishment enough?

Chapter 27

Nasreen Baji insisted I not leave the confines of our rooms the rest of the day. What more did she think Jawad Sahib would do? The numbness of the initial assault now faded, the bruise deepened into my skin, along with an anger so hot, it threatened to burn me alive.

Why did I take Nabila at her word? Why couldn't I have at least mentioned it to Mumtaz before I dashed off at the first opportunity?

There was no leaving this place.

There never would be.

"You weren't really running away, were you?" Nasreen Baji asked that evening.

"No, Baji."

"There are only so many times my son will let things pass. You must remember: You can't forget your place."

Forget my place? Every day I woke up without the scent of my mother's breakfast wafting through the air. Every day I woke to deafening silence instead of my sisters' laughter and shrieks. Every day I remembered everything I lost. I realized now that as kind as Nasreen Baji could be to me, she could never understand my position.

"I'm sorry," I said. "It will never happen again."

"Let me take a look at you." She motioned me toward her. "It will take a few days, but it will fade. I spoke with Jawad. He agrees you've been punished enough."

When she left to watch television in the living room that night, I returned to my room. No sooner did I sit down than the door creaked open. Fatima stepped inside. She carried a wooden tray with a bowl of lentils.

"Baba sent this for you." She set the tray down on my bed.

"Tell him I said thank you."

I saw a scrap of paper balled up in her fist.

"What's that?"

She handed the paper over shyly. I unfolded it. Line after line, an entire page was filled with the letter alif.

"Good work, Fatima! See how fast you learned?" I pulled

out a pencil from my satchel and turned the paper over. I drew the next letter. "It's curved like a cooking pot with a floating dot. You call it bey."

"Bey," she repeated.

I'd handed her the pencil to try it herself when the door opened again. Nabila and Mumtaz walked in.

"Nabila wants to say something to you," Mumtaz said. Nabila stood by the door, her arms limp at her sides.

"I'm sorry." Nabila glanced at Mumtaz and then back at me.

"It's done now," I said.

"It's just that everything was fine until you came here." Her lower lip quivered. "I served Baji loyally for years. I never complained. And now? She looks past me as if I don't exist."

"And the same will happen to me, too, one day, won't it?" I snapped. "I can't control it any more than you could."

"Amal's right. Nasreen chose to do what she did. It wasn't Amal's doing," Mumtaz said. "Nabila, jealousy will only hurt you. And, Amal, holding on to anger is useless. You both could be here forever, and the sooner you stop fighting and realize you are in the same situation, the easier your lives will be."

"You're right," Nabila said quietly. "I'm sorry."

"My head hurts," I said. "I'd like to rest."

Nabila searched my face before she followed Mumtaz and Fatima out of the room.

Forever.

Mumtaz said I could be here forever. I used to say the walk to the market took forever when the weather was especially hot. And that summers felt endless because I missed school. Only now that I was trapped did I understand the heaviness of forever.

If this was to be my life now, if this really was where I'd be stuck, then I did have to let go of what happened with Nabila. This was what my mother would tell me to do. She would tell me the only one I hurt by holding a grudge was myself. But how could I let it go? The thought seemed as impossible as leaving this gated estate behind me for good.

Chapter 28

I ironed and sorted Nasreen Baji's clothing the next day while she was out with her son visiting a prospective bride. Even though I knew Jawad Sahib wasn't here, stepping foot into the open foyer that afternoon left me feeling exposed.

Thankfully, the halls were empty right now.

I was walking down the hallway toward the main verandah to gather fresh flowers to replace the ones in her vases when I heard a knock on the front door.

Bilal hurried down the hallway and looked out the window.

"It's them again." He paled.

"Who?" I asked him.

"The p-police," he stammered. "But Jawad Sahib—he's gone. What do we do?"

The knocking resumed. Louder now.

Bilal glanced at me and bit his lip before he reached up and unlatched the door. Two police officers in dark green uniforms with brown batons and steel guns holstered at their waists sauntered into the marble foyer.

"Where is he?" the taller one asked Bilal.

"Jawad Sahib?" Bilal asked.

"Well, I'm not here to see you, am I?" the other officer retorted. His mustache was thick like bicycle handles. "Of course Jawad Sahib. Where is he?"

"He's not here." Bilal studied the ground. "He is out with his mother."

"When will they be back?"

"I'm not sure."

"Good timing." The taller officer smiled at the other one.

"I have a knack for these things." The mustached office grinned.

"No harm in taking a look around," the taller one said. "Might find some fun surprises along the way."

"We'll find what we need faster without him breathing down our neck, anyway," the other one said, and smirked.

How could they openly discuss wandering around

and disrupting Jawad Sahib's property? As if Bilal and I didn't exist?

These officers didn't care because it wouldn't be them Jawad Sahib would blame.

I expected Bilal to stop these men, whose muddy feet were already tracking footprints onto the marble floor, but he stood frozen to the side.

The officers wandered toward the hallway to the left of the spiral staircase, the one with the cream carpet, so difficult to clean.

No.

I was not going to let these police officers get us in trouble.

"Jawad Sahib will not be pleased if you walk around his house while he's not here," I called out.

"And who will tell him?" The taller one turned around and studied my face. "You'd be smart to remember he's not the only one who can leave bruises."

"If you have a message for him, I can relay it."

"My message is for you to mind your business. The guards understand this, and the boy over there definitely does. You'd be wise to follow their lead."

"Yes, go sweep the stairs, little girl. This doesn't concern you," the mustached one said.

"It does concern me." I pointed to their shoes. "You've tracked mud into the foyer, and once it gets to the carpet, I can't imagine anyone, especially Jawad Sahib, will be happy to see your footprints."

"She's right."

Jawad Sahib stood at the front door; Nasreen Baji clutched his arm.

"The girl misunderstood us," the tall one sputtered. "We were only inquiring where you were."

"And since when do you arrive unannounced?"

"Forgive us, but the orders came from above; our boss told us to get word to you immediately."

Jawad Sahib stared at them. "You'd be smart to remember you have more than one boss," he said.

"Yes, Jawad Sahib, you are right," the taller officer said.

The vein at the base of Jawad Sahib's neck throbbed. He strode to the backyard. The officers hurried after him.

"Well done, Amal," Nasreen Baji said. "That couldn't have been easy."

None of this is easy, I wanted to tell her.

My new life was simply about making choices, none of which I actually wished to make.

Chapter 29

I walked into the kitchen with Nasreen Baji's empty lunch tray that afternoon. When I stepped through the double doors, Hamid was patting down balls of dough while Fatima and Nabila were setting the servant plates and bowls onto the counter.

"Had a bit of flour left over, so I'm making us some fresh rotis," Hamid said when he saw me. He slapped a floured circle of dough onto the skillet and flipped it. "Get the food quick while it's nice and warm. We'll clean up after."

I hadn't had fresh rotis in so long. I quickly made myself a plate along with the other servants.

I trailed behind Mumtaz and sat down next to her.

"Is it true?" Hamid asked me when he joined us. "Did you really talk back to those officers?"

"She did," Bilal said. "I froze up as usual."

"No one blames you for being afraid around those monsters," Mumtaz said. "Not one bit."

"Were they the same police officers that came by last time?" Ghulam asked between bites.

"No," Bilal said. "These were different ones."

"It's a parade of them these days," Ghulam remarked.

Bilal shrugged and picked at his food. He didn't say anything. I was lucky I got to work for Nasreen Baji. I couldn't imagine having to cater to a person like Jawad Sahib.

I cleaned up my dishes and put them away. When I stepped into the hallway, Bilal and Nabila followed behind.

"Thank you." Bilal stuffed his hands in his kamiz. "Thank you for speaking up. You really saved me."

"Oh," I said. "That's okay. Really."

"Well, Nabila and I were talking." He glanced at her and then at me. "We know you like reading and were enjoying Jawad's library, weren't you?"

"It was a mistake," I said stiffly. "I shouldn't have done it."

"But what if you could read again?" Nabila asked.

I stared at her.

"Well, we were talking about it, and I know when he's here, when he's gone, and when he's coming back," Bilal said. "So maybe, if we were the lookout, you could borrow books again?"

"Why?" I asked. "Why would you help me?"

"Because we owe you," Nabila said. "It's our way to thank you."

"He would notice his books were missing," I said.

"Not if he forgot those books are even there. Come on," she said. "Follow us."

I trailed behind them down the hall to the library. Nabila walked over to one of the filing cabinets. She and Bilal pulled it forward to reveal a bookshelf wedged behind it.

"He jammed that new cabinet in there a few months back and hasn't moved it since. He probably doesn't even remember that there are books behind it."

I looked at Nabila. As tempting as the books were, how many times could I fall for her tricks?

"Amal," Nabila said. "I know I haven't made it easy. I'm sorry. But you can trust us, really. You're one of us now. As Mumtaz says, we have to look out for each other."

I looked at her and then at the books. I slipped out a thin collection of poems and short stories. I ran my hand over the cover.

I didn't expect to have this chance again—to be able to turn pages and learn new things and keep my mind alive.

I couldn't say no.

It was worth the risk to have books in my life again.

Chapter 30

$\mathcal{B}$ilal and Nabila remained true to their word. It had been one month since I began borrowing books from the library again. I'd gone through seven already. "You'll have a few hours now if you want to get a book," Bilal whispered to me now as we cleaned up after breakfast.

"Thanks," I told him. "I'll go in a few minutes."

I put away the breakfast tray and rinsed out the milk saucer before slipping into the library to get a book. I barely glanced at the title before cloaking it in my chador. My hands shook, waiting as I always did for someone to walk in on me, but no one did.

Nasreen Baji was resting when I stepped into her room,

so I had some time to read. I closed my door halfway and sat down on the bed.

I looked down at the book—*God's Own Land*—and turned to the first page.

"You think I might be able to read books like that one day?" a voice whispered.

I nearly leapt off the bed, but it was just Fatima. She lingered by the edge of the door.

"Yes." I gestured for her to close the door. "I know reading seems really complicated right now, but once you get the hang of it, it will be as easy as breathing."

"Could you read to me?" She took a step toward me.

"Well . . ." I looked down at the book. "This book is a little complicated."

"That's okay. I just want to hear it."

Fatima sat down next to me and I read to her.

I was wrong to expect her to get restless; instead she hung on to every word.

"Mumtaz and I are taking a break outside—join us?" Nabila asked me later that day, after Nasreen Baji had gone to visit a friend.

The thought of spending time with her still made me uneasy, but my mother's words from arguments with my sisters came to mind—you have to find a way to get along; you can't cast off your family. Nabila wasn't my family, but she was who I lived with now. I had to do my part and make peace.

I joined Nabila and Mumtaz on a charpai on the verandah. Rain drizzled down in the garden and a warm mist coated the air.

"Here, have some soda," Mumtaz said, handing us cola bottles. "Went to the store this morning for a few things. Figured you girls could use a treat."

"Thank you," I said.

"No shaking it this time, Nabila," Mumtaz said. "Remember what happened last time?"

"As if anyone lets me forget anything in this house!" Nabila exclaimed.

Mumtaz laughed and took a sip of tea.

"Did the soda erupt?" I asked.

"Yes. And how was I supposed to know it would sputter and fly out like that?" Nabila protested. "You shake up the mango juice and nothing happens—I figured it would be the same!"

"My sister made that mistake, too. She jumped up and down so much, the top flew off. Our ceiling is still stained from the fizzy soda."

"See?" Nabila smiled at me before turning to Mumtaz.

"I'm not the only one who's done that! It's a common mistake."

I smiled back at her. Nabila didn't need to know Safa was two years old when this happened.

I removed the metal top and took a sip of the frosty drink—the fizzy bubbles reminded me of my sisters' laughter.

"Can't remember the last time we had a good rainfall." Mumtaz nodded to the sky. "When I first came here, it seemed like my husband and I sat here all the time watching the raindrops dance."

"Your husband?"

"Yes. He was a gardener for the estate many years ago."

"You lived together here?"

"We lived with his family back then. But when my husband passed, I decided I'd rather live here."

How bad must it have been at her husband's home to choose this as a better alternative? But then I realized that Parvin had done the same thing. She lived in a shed behind our house instead of with her parents or her late husband's family. I had always assumed she came to live with us because she wanted to be near us, but perhaps it was more complicated than that.

"It's nice you're teaching Fatima to read," Nabila said.

"She's so proud of herself. Can't stop tracing the latest letter you taught her."

"I'm glad she's enjoying it," I said.

"It's not too late for you to learn to read," Mumtaz said, nudging Nabila. "I'm sure Amal could teach you."

"Yes, I could," I said, trying to hide my surprise that Nabila couldn't read. But it made sense. Nabila came when she was Fatima's age, and where would she have had the chance to keep up with whatever she might have learned before?

"Maybe," Nabila said, but she quickly changed the topic. "Did you hear the latest on the wedding drama?"

"I haven't." Mumtaz lowered her chai.

"The latest girl Nasreen Baji wants Jawad Sahib to see is Rashida's daughter!"

"Now, that's something." Mumtaz shook her head.

"Jawad was engaged to a cousin in that family," Nabila explained to me.

"He was engaged?"

"Well, barely. It only lasted two days. They didn't even announce it before he changed his mind," Mumtaz said.

"That's what he says," Nabila scoffed. "I heard she called it off when she heard about his temper. He was crushed."

"That's a foolish girl if that's true," Mumtaz said.

"Why?" I asked. "If she said no to him, she sounds like a smart girl to me."

"Nonsense," Mumtaz said. "This is a good life for someone who knows how to comport herself and is smart enough to figure him out."

"It's not fair," I said. "Why should anyone have to figure him out?"

"No, it's not fair. But that's life."

There it was yet again, my father's words: Life isn't fair. Maybe it was true, but why was that a reason to just accept everything and go along with it? I hoped the rumor about the girl turning down Jawad Sahib was true. I hoped there really was someone out there who had the courage to stand up to him and say no.

Chapter 31

Nasreen Baji shut the phone and sighed. She was sitting in the sunken living room next to Jawad Sahib as I handed her a cup of chai. The television was on low in the background.

"What's the matter?" Jawad Sahib asked.

"Zeba canceled our shopping trip to Lahore again."

"You probably don't want to go anyway," he said. "Traffic is terrible there these days."

"I need a new sari for your cousin's wedding, and I'm two seasons behind with all my clothes. But ever since Zeba's grandchild was born, she has no time."

"Go yourself, then."

"It's lonely traveling to the city alone. Come with me?"

She reached out and patted his hand. "We haven't done anything together in so long."

"You know how much work I have."

She frowned. Then she looked at me.

"That's it. Amal, you're coming with me," Nasreen said.

"Me?"

"It's a long drive, two hours if the traffic cooperates. Pack some dried snacks, water, and a thermos with chai."

Would Jawad Sahib interject? Tell her I couldn't leave the estate? He clicked on his phone and said nothing.

"Going to Lahore?" Nabila asked me when I walked into the kitchen.

"Yes, I need to get her snacks and tea in order," I said cautiously. Did she wish she was going instead of me? We'd gotten along fine in the months since our truce, but I couldn't completely forget her treachery.

"The bags get really heavy," she said. "By the end my arms usually feel like they'll fall off. Make sure to put the bags down every chance you get."

"Thanks for the tip," I said, and she smiled at me.

Sitting across from Nasreen Baji in the black town car that afternoon, we drove past cotton fields, orange groves, and sugarcane fields. Soon, my neighborhood snapped into view as we turned down the main street, the same one whose path I'd traveled nearly every week. We passed by the open-air market. Shaukat stood outside, talking to a kulfi vendor. I pressed my fingers against the darkened glass, watching the market slide past me, out of sight.

"Was that Shaukat?" Nasreen Baji asked.

"Yes," I said.

"For a second I thought it was his father. Things looked quiet there."

"It's not delivery day. On Tuesdays and Fridays, you can't find a spot to stand."

"Two shipments a week? That's impressive."

"They've added more space in the back. You can't see it from the road."

"I forget how it is with our villages. Only those who live there know exactly what is going on."

We drove past my street. And then, for a brief moment, my house flitted in and out of view. It looked smaller somehow. I wondered if all my memories of home would grow as distant as Nasreen Baji's had. Watching my village slip away in the rearview, I felt like I was losing a piece of myself.

. . .

I thought I knew what Lahore would be like, but it was one thing to read about it in a book or see it on television, and another to experience it for myself. Unlike the steady stream of the highway, here rickshaws, motorcycles, trucks, and cars shared the narrow roads alongside bicycles and throngs of people. Stores pressed against other stores on either side of us, large signs in Urdu and in English towering on billboards overhead.

Suddenly, the car jerked to a stop.

"We can't be there yet, can we?" Nasreen Baji asked Ghulam.

"Almost. It's another one of those protests blocking traffic."

"What's this one about?" She leaned against the car seat and sighed.

"Judge Barsi," he said as the car snaked slowly through the snarl of traffic. "That's what the signs say, anyhow."

I looked out the window. The sidewalks and streets up ahead were filled with people holding signs. Some had photos of the judge with angry red Xs splashed across his face.

A woman in a red hijab stood on a crate. She picked up a horn and shouted, "Jail Judge Barsi!" The crowd chanted along with her, and their voices made the car vibrate.

"So a judge does something they don't like and we pay the

price by sitting in traffic?" Nasreen Baji complained. "I swear, every week they find something new to get angry about."

I'd seen protests on the news, but seeing it in person, I felt the energy in the air. Even through the closed and darkened window it crackled through me.

At last, we reached the bazaar. I hopped out of the car and trailed behind Nasreen Baji through the arched entrance into the Anarkali bazaar. The smell of samosas and pakoras filled the air. In my old village there was one stall for all the snack foods. Here, stall after stall was lined up as far as I could see. Men shouted their prices over one another, and their voices echoed through the bazaar. We passed four different spice stores, each with turmeric and chilies lining the shelves and spices in colors and with names I had never seen before.

Streams of people brushed past us, and with the loud bargaining, the laughter, the arguing, and the honking of cars in the distance, everything felt like it was merging into one beating pulse.

And the people. Some girls were dressed like me in plain shalwar kamizes. Other girls wore pants and blouses. I saw some fully covered with nothing but their eyes revealed, while others wore short-sleeved shirts.

All this time I'd wanted to travel to faraway cities, but here, just a few hours away, was Lahore, another planet.

We passed a shoe store, a handbag store, and a shop where rows and rows of bangles lined the walls. I wanted to take a moment and absorb everything, but I had to keep up with Nasreen Baji as she hurried toward the sari shop.

Stepping inside, I stood against the back wall. Nasreen Baji sat down on a red cushioned pillow and pointed to the rows of fabric lining the walls. The shopkeepers pulled off the bolts of silk and unfurled them across the floor in front of her. Soon the floor was a sea of green, sky blue, and petal pink. It would take hours for them to put everything back in place, but the men didn't seem to care. Nasreen Baji sifted through the different saris and picked three.

I had never seen anyone shop with the freedom of Nasreen Baji. After the sari shop, she walked into store after store and simply pointed to what she liked—gold earrings, silver heeled shoes, ruby-encrusted bangles—and just like that, they became hers.

The sun was beginning to set when we got into the car. Nabila was right about the heavy bags—my arms strained from the weight of them.

The sky flushed pink, then deepened into purple as we drove. It was fully set when we passed our villages. I looked at my school under the glow of the moon. Hafsa's house.

My own.

"You didn't tell me Shabnum is getting married," Nasreen Baji said.

"Shabnum?" I repeated. That was Hafsa's oldest sister.

"Shaukat's daughter. This weekend. Borrowed some money for her dowry, even though it'll still be a modest one, given their financial circumstances. Your family never mentioned it?"

"I don't have a phone," I told her.

"Everyone has a phone. Why didn't you bring one?"

"Jawad Sahib took mine when I first arrived."

"You mean to tell me you haven't spoken to your family since you came?"

I shook my head.

"Your poor mother, she must be so worried!" Her eyes widened. "That settles it. She deserves to see for herself that you're all right. You can have three days. Attend the festivities and spend some time with your family."

"Would Jawad Sahib let me?"

"Why wouldn't he?" she asked. "You have time off. It's entitled to you."

I'd lived at their estate long enough, but there was still so much I didn't understand. But those thoughts were quickly replaced by thoughts of home. How badly did

I miss the familiar curve of my bed? My mother's food? Seema and my little sisters? My friends?

I knew I should thank Nasreen Baji. Tell her how much this meant to me. But how could I possibly express my gratitude? Words failed.

I could go home. However briefly, I could go home.

Chapter 32

"Can't you drive faster?" I asked Ghulam.

"I'm driving no slower and no faster than I ever do," he replied.

"But a little faster wouldn't hurt anyone! Please?"

"You're going to pay the cost to fix this car if something happens to it?" He laughed.

"Ghulam Baba," I pleaded. "Just this once?"

He shook his head, but he glanced at me in the rearview mirror and winked. The engine hummed louder, and the scenery passed faster now. Soon, my neighborhood sprang into view. Water buffalo roamed the distant fields. A group of boys kicked a faded soccer ball in the street. The car jerked to a stop. Children pointed at it and blocked its path.

I pushed the door open.

Ghulam rolled down his window.

"What are you doing?" he asked. "It's just one block over!"

"I can't wait!" I shouted. "Thanks for the ride!" I broke into a run down the road. There it was. The rosebushes. The worn front door creaked when I opened it, like always.

As I stepped inside, it felt like the past few months had been a terrible nightmare. And now it was over.

I was home.

Safa and Rabia stood by the couch; they were so engrossed in their argument, they didn't see me at first. I took in their flushed cheeks and hands on their hips as their complaints echoed off the concrete walls.

Seema peeled a cucumber by the stove. She turned to hush them. That's when she saw me. She gasped. Her knife clattered to the ground.

"Amal!" she shouted. She rushed toward me and wrapped me in a hug. I had forgotten what it was like to feel someone's embrace.

"Baji's here!" Rabia and Safa shrieked in unison. Their eyes lit up like a string of lights on Eid. They dashed toward me. I picked them both up and hugged them. I didn't know how I would ever let go.

"Amal?"

My mother. She carried my little sister Lubna in her arms. Her hair was loose and damp, grayer than it had been three months earlier. She walked toward me and stroked my hair as if checking to make sure I was real. Then, her expression crumbled. She folded me into her arms.

"They said I could come for a few days." I hugged her. "For the wedding. I can't believe I'm home right now!"

"I called you. Every day. The phone rang without answer, and then one day it stopped ringing altogether. Had to wait the longest time before I could get word you were all right." She wiped tears from her eyes.

"He took my phone. The first day. I've been desperate to talk to you. To all of you."

"Seema, get your father," my mother said. "Amal, sit here. Let me get a good look at you."

Despite the exhaustion lining her face, she looked like my mother again.

"Our dolls missed you," Rabia said, holding out her patchwork doll to me. Safa hurried over with hers as well. They talked over each other, sharing all the adventures I missed. I marveled at Safa's words, the first time I'd heard her speak so clearly. Lubna was a plump baby now, with soft curls like Safa's and Rabia's. I held out my hands to pick her up, but she pulled back, studying me shyly from my mother's arms. She had no memories of gripping my hand and looking into my eyes all those hours when she was a newborn. I was not an older sister to her. I was a stranger.

"How are you doing there? In that house?" my mother asked.

I fidgeted in my seat. I waited so long to come here. To let go of everything weighing on my heart. But the thing was, she looked so happy to see me. After everything I put her through, how could I add more burdens on her back?

"Nasreen Baji treats me well," I managed to say. "I'm lucky I work for her."

"Good." She exhaled. "I know it's not easy, but I know how strong you are."

Strong? What did it mean to be strong? Did I have any other choice?

Before I could say anything more on this, the front door opened.

My father stepped inside. He walked straight over to me and hugged me, his face wet with tears. With his arms around me, for the first time since I came home, I cried.

The room grew quiet when I pulled away.

"I'm sorry." I wiped my eyes.

"Don't be," my mother said. "You are free here."

The door opened again. "I thought my ears were playing tricks on me."

Parvin! I raced over to hug her.

"Where is Omar?"

"Oh, Amal." She winced. "He's at orientation this weekend."

"Orientation?"

"Yes, for the boarding school, remember?"

I remembered now. Our conversation by the stream. It felt like a lifetime ago now.

"He starts in the fall, and they wanted the new students to come spend the weekend there to get acquainted. He's going to be so upset he missed your visit."

"I'm so glad things are moving along with that," I told her.

And I was. If my own future had to be yanked away, at least Omar had one.

We ate dinner in the courtyard that night. I fixed myself a plate of kardhai chicken and the fresh wheat roti my mother had made minutes earlier. I had no idea how badly I missed my mother's food until I took a bite; Hamid was a good cook, but there was nothing in the world that could compare to my mother's food.

"Did you know I'm learning to read?" Rabia told me.

"Seema's teaching her." My mother nodded. "She'll start school in a few weeks."

"When can I start?" Safa frowned.

"When you can behave!" Rabia stuck out her tongue.

Seema interceded to cut off their argument. My mother grabbed Safa and put her in her lap.

When the conversation turned to the preparations for Hafsa's sister's wedding, everyone started talking at once, and I found it difficult to focus. I felt overwhelmed by the laughter, chatter, and squeals of my sisters—the sounds that I had missed so much. I tried to still myself and soak it all in, to hold on to when I was gone.

I used to complain to Omar about my chaotic home. I took any opportunity to escape to the sugarcane fields when the noise became too much. Why did I get so annoyed at the sound of my sisters' chatter? Why did I get frustrated with my chores? Why did it take leaving my ordinary life behind to appreciate how precious it truly was?

"Okay, girls," my mother said when the last of the rotis vanished from the hot pot. "Seema, watch the baby while I get the girls ready for bed?"

"I can do it," I said.

"Nonsense. You're our guest here for a short while. Relax."

Guest?

It was just an offhand remark.

They meant it kindly.

But to call me a guest in the only place I ever belonged—the word cut like a jagged stone against my heart.

Chapter 33

I helped Safa and Rabia put on their matching yellow frocks for the mehndi. Tonight was the first of the wedding festivities, and it was my favorite day because unlike the actual wedding ceremony tomorrow, which could be a bit somber, the mehndi was a happy celebration where everyone danced, sang, and decorated each other's hands and feet with henna.

"Thanks for getting the girls dressed," my mother said as she stepped into our room. "Here are your outfits." She handed Seema and me our freshly pressed clothes.

I put on the orange silk kamiz and green churidar pajamas that I'd worn to my cousin's wedding late last year. After so long wearing simple cotton, this fabric felt smooth and light against my skin.

"You look pretty," Seema said. "Orange always looks good on you."

"So do you," I told her. "I don't remember your outfit. Did Amma have it dyed a different color from when it was mine?"

"No. This outfit is new!" She grinned. "The tailor measured me twice to make sure it fit just right!"

"It's beautiful," I said. I was glad Seema got to wear an outfit that was all her own, but knowing the reason why—because she had replaced me as the eldest in my family—saddened me, too.

Our conversation was interrupted by a knock on the front door.

"Amal!"

I knew the voice before I turned around. It was Hafsa!

"You're back!" She hugged me. "I just heard. I knew your father would come up with the money! I knew he would!"

"I'm only here for the weekend," I said.

"Oh." Her smile faded.

Hafsa grew quiet and glanced at Seema and then back at me.

"Well, I'm glad you're here now," she finally said. "How've you been?"

"It's been hard, but I'm managing," I said.

"Oh," she said.

There it was again, that unfamiliar silence. I waited for her to ask me about the estate. About Jawad Sahib and what it was like to live there. Here I was with all the first-hand information she could ever dream of, but instead, the quiet continued to stretch between us while she studied the ground.

I cleared my throat. "How's Miss Sadia?"

"She's good!" Hafsa perked up. "But she still goes over our class time."

"Yeah." Seema nodded. "Some things don't change. Especially around here."

"Well, except for that building, right?" Hafsa said to Seema. She turned to me. "It opens next week. We were all wrong, weren't we?"

"What building?"

"The one with the green door," she said. "I was right— Khan Sahib's family was building it, but it wasn't a factory. It's a literacy center."

So the center Nasreen Baji had bragged about to her friend was the mysterious building we watched go up. And it was in my own village.

"No one's going to go," Hafsa said. "They don't want to touch anything that family is involved with."

"But it's free, isn't it?" I said.

"Nothing with him is free," Hafsa said. "You of all people know that."

"Hafsa?" my mother said as she walked into the room. "Your mom just called. She was looking for you."

"Oops," she said. "I better go. Get there on time, okay? Farah and I are going to do a dance!"

Before I could respond, she raced out the door.

How quickly her life had moved on.

While I scraped plates and massaged migraines, she practiced dance steps with our classmate Farah. They got to go to school and dream about a future. I knew Hafsa missed me and cared about me, but she got to barrel forward, her life uninterrupted, while my future had fallen completely off its tracks.

Would Farah be Hafsa's roommate someday?

Chapter 34

Pink, green, and yellow lights illuminated the tent Hafsa's parents erected behind their home for the mehndi.

I stepped onto the carpeted floor of the tent with my family. My father wandered over to the folding chairs set up outside the tent for the men under the night sky. Rabia and Safa held tight to my kamiz as if I might vanish without warning.

The bride, Hafsa's eldest sister, Shabnum, sat perched on a cushioned stage in the center of the tent. A yellow veil framed her face, and her hands were already covered with henna patterns. Now the henna artist was swirling intricate designs of flowers and birds onto her feet.

We walked over to sit on the cushions below Shabnum's

stage. I smiled a little at how subdued she seemed. Hafsa and her sisters were *not* the docile sort, but the bride was doing her best to look the part for the occasion.

Seema picked up a henna cone left out for the guests to use and began swirling it on my hand.

"Are you done?" I asked her after a while. "My hand is aching!"

"Be patient. I have to get the pattern right! You squirm too much."

"Sorry." I tried to still myself. The designs on my palms would take hours to dry, but tomorrow the deep brown Seema painted on would transform into a brilliant orange. It would eventually fade away completely, but for a little while, when I was back at Jawad Sahib's estate, these hands would remain colored with the memory of this night.

A new song started up, and I watched Hafsa and Farah dance with a third girl. It was Sana—Nasreen Baji's niece. Their braids were woven with marigolds, and they wore matching outfits.

Chatter swirled around me. Gossip about the groom. The dowry.

"You poor dear," a woman said to me. It was Hira, the butcher's wife. She settled next to me and tucked her feet under herself. "Everyone is beside themselves about you having to live in the same place as that monster."

"What's it like there?" another woman asked. "Drove by the place once, but you can't even see the roof from the road."

"It's those walls he's got," my neighbor Balkis interjected. "Walls and bushes to keep everyone far away."

"Does he have a waterfall in the house?" Hira asked me.

"No, there's no waterfall," I said.

"I knew a woman who worked for them years ago. Told me about a waterfall right in their living room."

"Heard about the gold staircases, too." Balkis nodded.

"Now, that Nasreen . . ." Hira clucked her tongue. "Came from the village over on the other side of the market but thinks she's something else now. Doesn't even bother to see her family anymore."

"She's nice," I interrupted. "She's been good to me. She really has."

But they continued their conversation as though I hadn't spoken. I watched their animated expressions and listened to the theories of Nasreen Baji's past and the details of the estate.

Seema squeezed my wrist. "Ignore them," she said. "They're just gossiping."

She was right. For these women, my circumstances were a juicy story. One they could whisper about and cluck their tongues over before moving on to other things.

They didn't have to tiptoe around Jawad Sahib.

They didn't have to be wrenched away from everyone they loved.

They weren't bad people. They were just lucky enough to have no idea of the reality I faced.

Chapter 35

Ghulam would be here to pick me up any minute. As I packed boxes of my favorite biscuits into my suitcase for Fatima and the others, there was a knock on the door. Seema went to open it, but instead of Ghulam, it was Fozia.

"I brought these for you," Fozia said. She stepped inside with a box of yellow laddus. She set it on the table.

"Thank you. I've missed your sweets," I said.

"Seema," my mother said, "can you get a plate for them?"

"No, no, they're for Amal. I know how much she loves them," Fozia said. "I came to say goodbye, and I had a question." She hesitated. "I heard you work for Nasreen. Do you think if you talked to her about something, she might listen?"

"Why?" I asked her. "What happened?"

Fozia shook her head and squeezed her eyes shut. Tears slipped down her cheeks.

"Tell me, please." I grabbed her hands. "What's wrong?"

"It's ever since we replaced that roof. And then we needed a little more to fix our freezer. And then there was the wedding. We're paying as much as we can each month, but when his officer came to collect last time, he said if we don't increase our payments soon, he'll take drastic measures. But we can't pay any more than we already are. We can't!"

"Fozia," my mother said. "Amal is a servant in their home. What power do you think she has? Look how indebted we are."

There was the sound of a car pulling up, and the back door creaked open. Seema rushed into the living room as my father stepped inside. "Ghulam is outside, but he said you could take your time."

Fozia stood. "I don't know what I was thinking." She looked at my mother and me. "Except if there was a chance, I had to ask."

"I know." My mother hugged her.

I blinked back tears after Fozia left. "I wish I could help her."

"Amal, even if you could help them, imagine who else

will come to you for the same," my mother said. She put her arm around me.

It was then I noticed her arms were bare.

"Where are your gold bangles?" I asked.

My mother glanced at my father.

"She sold them," he said.

But those bangles were as much a part of my mother as her long wavy hair. I couldn't remember a moment she didn't have them on.

"It's the first thing we did when you left," Seema said. "We were sure we could work something out, but even with her wedding jewelry, the tractor, the television . . . Even if we sold them all, it wouldn't be enough. Not even close."

I looked at my mother, at my sisters. Seema's arms were crossed, her face ashen. They had tried everything they could think of to get me back and failed. So if they were continuing with their lives, it was because they had no other choice. Just like me.

"I'm not leaving that place, am I?" I whispered to my father.

I waited for him to answer my question. Instead, he hugged me tight.

I hugged the rest of my family goodbye. My mother. My sisters. I kissed the baby. She smiled at me and cooed, but I knew I would soon be a stranger to her again.

I thought coming home would help me feel better, but now all I could see was my mother's bare wrists, Fozia's frightened face, and a baby sister who would never know me. How many lives had this man upended?

Why did no one stop him?

Chapter 36

It felt strange to be back at the Khan estate. The marble tiles, immaculate white hallways, and enormous windows devoid of dust or fingerprints—none of this was foreign anymore.

Nasreen had smiled when I brought her tea upon my return. Nabila admired my intricate orange henna designs, and Fatima hugged me and didn't let go until she extracted a promise of a lesson as soon as our work was done.

It was strange to step into this house and not feel terrified. To see people who welcomed me back. It wasn't long ago I was completely alone here.

I pressed Nasreen Baji's clothing that night and hung them in her armoire while she reclined on her bed and listened to me describe the wedding. She asked me about the tent and the decorations, and the type of jewels in Shabnum's wedding necklace. As I described the velvet wedding dress in full detail, and the satchels of dates and almonds the groom's family passed out for each guest, it almost felt like I was gossiping with a friend. "The purse she carried was so tiny that it looked like a small fan, but it was big enough to hold all the gift envelopes," I told her. "My sister Seema joked it had to have invisible layers hidden within to keep it expanding."

"Was my sister there?" she asked.

"Yes. And I saw your niece Sana. She danced with my friends at the wedding."

"Last time I saw Sana, she couldn't crawl—now she's dancing?"

"Crawl?" I asked. "But she's Seema's age. You haven't seen her in . . ."

"Eleven years," she said. "Time gets away from you."

"But it's your family!" I bit my tongue. I shouldn't have said anything, but how could she find time to go to Lahore for shopping trips and not have time to see her family who lived just ten minutes away?

"I want to see them," she said quietly. "Used to go once a week when I first got married. But after a while, Khan Sahib thought it was best his wife not mingle with villagers, and I agreed. But he takes care of them. Makes sure they want for nothing . . ."

Nasreen Baji had a bedroom that was practically the size of my house and the finest food and clothing. But she couldn't see the people she wanted to see the most.

Her cage was nicer than mine, but it was still a cage.

I cleared my throat. "I brought something for you." I went into my room and returned with a box.

"What's this?" She smiled.

"Laddus. I thought you might like them."

"They look homemade!"

"My neighbor Fozia made it. Shaukat's wife." It felt strange saying Fozia's name in this estate, remembering how frightened she had looked.

"I haven't had a homemade laddu since I was a child."

"She's known for her sweets. Her daughter is one of my best friends."

Nasreen Baji lifted a yellow confection from the box and took a bite. She closed her eyes.

"Do you like it?"

She fell silent for a few seconds. "It tastes like home," she said.

A knock on the bedroom door interrupted us. Jawad Sahib stepped inside.

"He keeps calling me!" he said. He waved his phone at Nasreen Baji. "Five missed calls while I'm in the shower."

"Jawad," Nasreen Baji sighed.

"You'd think I have nothing else to do but cater to his demands!"

"Well, if you helped him with the center, he wouldn't call so much," Nasreen Baji said. "He needs you. This literacy center is going to get him more votes for the next election, but only if people attend it."

"Why is that my problem? I have more than enough of my own things to deal with! And I have better things to do than force people to attend a ridiculous center."

"Jawad, if a journalist comes snooping and finds no one there, it could hurt your father's election campaign. And that affects all of us. The school can sit empty after the election for all it matters. If we don't get at least one person there by next week, the teacher said he's going to leave."

Jawad Sahib exhaled loudly, and then his eyes settled on mine.

"What about her?"

"What do you mean?"

"She can go to the center." He laughed at her astonished expression. "It's not such a far-fetched idea," he said. "We'll send her once a week. The center will officially have a student, and the teacher will have something to do. Problem solved."

"Jawad, it's a literacy center for adults."

"Better her than no one at all."

Me? Attend a literacy center? That meant I could see a teacher again. Maybe they could show me how to write the poem I had wanted to write months earlier. Maybe they had books I could borrow. I studied Nasreen Baji, not daring to hope, but then—

"Fine," she said. "Until we can get some actual other people to start going, she can attend."

Chapter 37

Ghulam dropped me off at the curb of the school. The bright yellow building with the green door was so different from the gray and brick structures I was accustomed to. I liked its color. It was the color of hope.

The interior smelled of fresh paint; soft overhead lights lent warmth to the space. A girl with two braids tied with ribbons sat at a desk in a reception area with a patchwork sofa and a coffee table scattered with magazines.

"Here for class?" the girl asked. She twirled a pencil between her fingers. She looked familiar—perhaps our paths had crossed at the market or she was the relative of a neighbor or a friend. Everyone here seemed to be connected in some way.

"Yes. My name is Amal."

"Oh, right. We're expecting you." She stood up and led me down the hall to a classroom, where a young man greeted me.

"Ah, our first student!" he said. "My name is Asif. I'll be your teacher."

"It's a big classroom," I said, looking around a large room that held a few wooden tables and chairs.

"Well, hopefully it won't seem so empty once we get more students," he said.

"The way you talk," I said. "It's unusual."

"My accent." He laughed. "I went to college in the United States; I guess some sort of accent stuck. My wife teases me about it, but I thought she was joking until now."

"Sorry to mention it," I said, flustered. "It's not bad. I like it."

"Thanks." He smiled and pushed the notebook toward me. "So today, we're doing a diagnostic exam. It tells me what you know and what we can work on. Don't worry about getting it all right—we use this to plan your lessons."

I opened the notebook and picked up the freshly sharpened pencil. It smelled like math tests and poetry and all the dreams I once took for granted.

Then I looked at the first page.

"This is the alphabet," I said.

"Very good! And by month's end, you will know it all! Go ahead and read out loud for me each one you know and circle the ones you don't."

Of course it was the alphabet. I got so excited to be in a learning center and meet a teacher again that I forgot this was a place to teach people how to read. I wasn't here to learn. I was window dressing in case someone came by.

"Don't worry about getting it wrong," he encouraged. "Mistakes happen. If you knew everything, there'd be no point in being here."

"That's the thing," I said. "I know all my letters."

"Well, that's what the diagnostic is for. If you know your letters, we can move on to connecting them. And then we can start on books. By the end of this program, you won't just know your letters; you'll be reading whole books."

He picked up a basket of books and set them on the table. Pictures of kittens and puppies smiled up at me. I looked at the one on top. It was the story of the cat that raised mice. The same story I read to Safa and Rabia not long ago.

"The last book I finished was Benazir Bhutto's biography," I said.

"Bhutto's biography?" His smile faded. "I don't understand. If you can read, why did they send you here?"

The silence stretched between us. When he spoke again, his words were flat.

"Let me guess. The man who paid for this center is running for office?"

I nodded.

"So this was a publicity stunt, and you're here in case a journalist shows up and reports on an empty building?"

If I said yes, would he tell Jawad Sahib?

"This isn't the first time," he sighed before I had a chance to reply. "Well, whatever the reason, there are plenty of people here who need this center. I spent the morning taping flyers on nearly every door in this and the other neighboring villages. It just takes one person to get the community to warm up."

"They won't come."

"Why wouldn't they?" He looked startled. "It's all right. You can tell me," he said, noticing my worried expression. "Why wouldn't they come?"

"I won't get in trouble?" I asked.

"You won't. I promise. Please tell me."

"Because everyone is scared of Jawad Sahib. They're scared to come into his center."

"But this isn't *his* center," he said. "His family sponsored the building and helped pay for the startup costs, but everything else—my salary, the materials, the books—it's all funded by the Ministry of Education."

"The people here don't care who paid for what. The

Khan family's name is attached to it and that's all they need to know."

"Well, that's just great." He pulled up his laptop. He opened a bright white screen with a small box and typed. Words transformed with the touch of his fingers on the keyboard.

"Is that an email?"

He turned to look at me.

"I wasn't reading it." I blushed. "It's just . . . I've seen people do that before on television. Nasreen Baji does it, too."

"Yes." He turned back to the screen. "I'm letting the people back at headquarters know what the situation is. See what we can do."

"How much faster is it to send a message this way than through the postal service?"

He laughed, but when he saw my expression, he cleared his throat. "It's definitely faster than the postal service. Want to pull up a chair? I can show you how it works."

When I sat next to him, he explained how people had email addresses just like they had home addresses. You could send messages from your own email address to other people with email addresses, and whatever you wrote came to the other person in a matter of seconds. It was like a telephone for words.

"That must make life so much easier," I said.

"Yes." He paused and studied me. "Want me to show you some more about computers?"

"Really?"

"Sure," he said. "We have an hour. May as well teach someone something." He pulled up a blank page with colored squares lining the side. "Ignore the English letters—I'm just showing you how to use the mouse to click and drag. The basics." He clicked on a pink square. Then he clicked on the white space and drew a pink circle. He clicked on a black square and dotted two eyes. With the green he dotted a nose. With the blue, a smile.

"See?" he said. "Easy. Now copy me."

"Drawing a face?" I laughed.

"A computer is simple once you get the hang of it, but you have to get the basics down," he said. "It may seem silly to draw a picture, but it's the simple things that pave the road for the rest of it."

The rest of the hour vanished as I copied his drawings. We tried more complicated shapes. I learned to click. To drag. To drop.

"I might be able to find some reading or math software for you next time you come," he said.

"Thank you so much." I glanced back at the basket. "Would it be okay if I borrowed a book?"

"One of those?" He laughed. "I think you'll find those a little dull if you've been reading Iqbal."

"Not for me," I said. "For Fatima—she's a child who works at the estate. I'm teaching her to read."

"A fellow teacher." He smiled and handed me a book. "Of course."

A fellow teacher—me? I almost laughed, but he was right. I might not have had my own classroom, but I was teaching Fatima. So I *was* a teacher.

I walked out of the center with a smile on my face. I had forgotten how my mind buzzed after a lesson. I'd forgotten how each answer my teachers gave led to ten new questions. I'd forgotten how alive it all made me feel.

My new teacher had given me a reason to dream again.

Chapter 38

I have a surprise for you," I told Fatima the next evening.

I had left Nasreen Baji watching television in the living room and slipped into the kitchen, where Fatima was putting the leftovers from the evening meal in the fridge.

"Surprise?" Fatima squinted at me.

I pulled out the book from behind my back.

"A book?" Her eyes widened. "Could I read it?"

"Well, maybe some of the words!" I said. "Want to read together? We can see which ones you can try to sound out."

Fatima hurried over to me as I turned to the first page. I read her the story of a lion and a mouse. The lion saved the mouse, and as the story continued, the mouse saved the lion in return. I watched her mouth form some of the words in disbelief. Sure, the words were simple, but it was happening. Fatima was learning to read.

"Fatima! You're doing it! See how many words you knew?"

Fatima beamed.

The doorbell chimed. I shut the book and glanced at the clock. It was just after dinner. People never came at this hour.

Fatima and I stepped out of the kitchen and walked down the hallway to the foyer. We saw Bilal hurrying to the front door. He looked out the window. His hand tightened on the doorknob before opening it. I knew before he opened it. It was the police again.

Nasreen Baji strode toward the door as the two officers stepped into the foyer. They were different from the ones who came last time.

"I apologize for disrupting you at this late hour," the bearded officer said. "We need to speak with Jawad Sahib. It's an urgent matter, and we are unable to reach him by phone."

"He's not home," Nasreen Baji replied.

"Where might he be?"

"I'm not sure."

"His own mother doesn't know where he is," the other officer muttered.

"Excuse me?" She raised her voice. "Do you think we enjoy these regular intrusions? Khan Sahib will not be amused when he finds out how late at night you came to harass his wife."

"I apologize for Usman," the bearded officer interjected. He handed her a card. "It's just that it's important we speak to him."

"I will relay the message."

Her face remained stony until they walked out of the foyer.

"They've never done that before," she exclaimed once they were gone. "They would never dare." She looked at the card. "What on earth is going on?"

She picked up her phone.

"I need to make some calls," she said to me. "Go look and see if anything needs to be done in the kitchen."

She headed up the stairs to her bedroom.

"Can you read the book to me again?" Fatima tugged at my kamiz.

"Tomorrow."

"One last time? Please?"

We slipped back into the kitchen. She listened, not moving a muscle as I read to her again.

When I finished, Fatima leaned up and kissed my cheek. "Thank you," she said.

I knew learning to read wouldn't change the fact that Fatima was trapped here like I was, cleaning floors, dusting baseboards, and peeling potatoes. But at least by teaching her to read, I gave her a window to see worlds beyond ours and a chance to imagine leaving the walls of this estate and to feel free, even if it was only for a little while.

Chapter 39

Asif was already sitting at the desk at the literacy center, typing on his laptop, when I walked into his classroom. His eyebrows were knit in concentration. He nodded when he saw me. I sat down across from him and pushed the book I'd borrowed across the table to him.

"Thank you for lending me the book," I told him.

"How did she like it?" he asked.

"She loved it! She made me read it so many times this morning, I think she's memorized the story."

"That's great." He smiled. "I have some easier ones you can take for her today. She might even be able to read those all the way through on her own, based on the letters and sounds she knows. And good news! I found some great software that teaches math and reading. I've ordered it for the center, and it should be here in time for our next session."

"Really? Thank you so much!"

"While we wait for it to come in, I thought you could practice how to take a multiple-choice online test. I found a few basic reading passages. They're a little silly, but they'll do the job while we wait for the software."

He pushed the laptop toward me and pulled his chair next to me.

A giggle escaped when I saw the screen. An elephant, a dog, a cat, and a mouse grinned at me on-screen.

"I warned you." Asif laughed.

I clicked on the green arrow. It opened a new page with the story.

> *The elephant chases the dog.*
> *The dog chases the cat.*
> *The cat chases the mouse.*
> *The mouse chases the ant.*
> *The ant chases the elephant,*
> *and around and around they go.*

"Okay, now that that's done"—he rolled his eyes—"let's go to the multiple-choice part. Click the prompt below. It will open a smaller screen with the questions."

I stared at the screen.

"Amal? Something wrong?"

"It's cruel."

"What do you mean?"

"This poem. It's trying to say there is always someone to go after someone and keep the balance of power equal. But it's not true. The elephant is in control. The mouse. The cat. The ant. They can do what they like, but sooner or later they will all be gone except the elephant. Pretending otherwise is foolish."

"There is a saying: Elephants fear no other animal but ants. Who is to say if it's true or not, but—"

"It's not true. The biggest are not afraid of the smallest. In the end, the biggest wins."

"The story is trying to teach young children about justice and fairness . . ."

"But life isn't fair! I will be a servant for the rest of my life because I spoke back to the wrong person. I will be indebted to him my entire life. I was going to be a teacher. I was going to go to college. All my dreams are gone because one person has the power to crush them. And guess what happened to the last group of people who tried to stop him? He burned their village to the ground. I saw the deserted village with my own eyes. They lost everything, and Jawad Sahib? He gained more. The bigger always have all the power. They aren't scared of the little people. It just doesn't work like that."

My hands shook. I placed them on the desk to steady myself. Why did a silly poem affect me so much? I moved to apologize, but he spoke first.

"Amal, I'm sorry. I had no idea of your circumstances. But even in difficult situations, *especially* in difficult situations, you can't lose hope. Things change. They might even change for you one day."

He said it with such conviction, he could have fooled me if I didn't know better.

"My great-grandfather was a judge," he continued. "My grandfather was a lawyer. My father is a lawyer. He's argued cases in front of the highest courts. When I told him I wanted to be a teacher, he laughed at me. Then he threatened to defund my education. But I held strong. I found a way. I'm the first one to be a teacher in my family. No one supported me, but I did it because this is what I always wanted to do. If I thought nothing would change, nothing ever would. I know the situation is different, but things can change even when you don't think they will."

"You're from a big city," I said. "It's different here."

"That's not true. Things are changing in villages all over the country, even here." He hesitated before adding, "Especially here."

He minimized the poem on the screen and clicked a new website. He typed for a moment, and then a news story flashed across the screen.

Salim Mushtaq Still Missing as Local Landlord Is Investigated

A photo of Jawad Sahib stared back at me.

"The son of a diplomat disappeared not far from here," Asif explained. "Apparently, he's one of quite a few to go missing around here. But considering who he is, and that election season is approaching, the police are forced to take it seriously, and they're looking into Jawad Sahib's possible involvement."

I stared at the eyes gleaming back at me from the screen.

"No one would have bothered to investigate a family like the Khans even a few years ago," Asif said. "But people all around the country are fighting the status quo. Things *are* changing."

I hoped what Asif was saying was true, but I found it hard to believe. Asif couldn't understand how things worked here and the absolute power a family like the Khans held in a place like ours.

Chapter 40

Nabila, Bilal, and I lingered by the door to the main verandah, watching Nasreen. She sat on a wicker chair, the tea in her hands long cold, a folded newspaper resting on her lap.

"What's going on?" Nabila asked. "I've never seen her like this."

"Jawad's been gone for days and hasn't returned a single call," Bilal replied.

"I heard her this morning," I admitted. "She also left a message for her husband. She was so upset, I thought she might cry."

"Jawad Sahib is in some sort of trouble," Bilal said. "I

think that's why he doesn't take me along with him on his trips anymore. He thinks if he doesn't take me, I won't find out what's going on."

"I read a news article about it," I whispered. "They are investigating if he had something to do with a missing person."

"Who was it?" Nabila asked me. "It had to be someone important to have the police poking their noses around here so much."

"Enough." Mumtaz appeared and frowned at us. "I hope you are not gossiping about the hands that feed us," she said. "It's not our concern what they might be up to."

Nabila glanced at me and rolled her eyes, but before she could say anything else, the front door thudded; Nasreen Baji's eyes widened when Jawad Sahib stepped onto the verandah. He was accompanied by a man with a shock of white hair and a thick mustache, wearing a white shalwar kamiz. Nasreen Baji jumped up and rushed toward them.

"You're home!" she exclaimed. "Never thought I'd see the day."

"Needed to sort out this police business once and for all," the man replied. "I'll be paying them a personal visit today."

"Mumtaz, go and air out Khan Sahib's wardrobe," Nasreen Baji said.

"No need. I have to leave this evening."

"What?" Her expression drooped. "After all this time away, you can't even stay the night?"

"You don't know the pressures I'm under. The federal police are on my back. They're not as simple to shake off as the ones here. Although they've gotten worse here, too." He glared at Jawad Sahib. "I keep you here to handle things, and I expect them to be handled. Never thought you'd make more problems for me."

"Is this is about that missing boy?" She held up her newspaper. "Why did I have to read about it in the papers like a common villager?"

"I told you already," Jawad Sahib said. "I don't want you to have to concern yourself with this."

"Well, it's hard not to concern myself when ill-mannered police officers charge into our house. I've never been so disrespected."

"They dared to be rude to you?" Khan Sahib's face reddened.

"Yes. Why do you think I've been trying to call you both so many times?" Nasreen turned to her son. "You could have at least sent me a message to let me know you were all right, Jawad. The way they barged in—can you imagine what went through my mind?"

"I'm sorry," Jawad Sahib said.

"I will take care of it," Khan Sahib told her. "They won't bother you again."

"And the things they're saying in the papers . . ." Nasreen Baji shook her head. Her eyes watered.

"Jawad says none of it is true," Khan Sahib said. "That boy comes by to see Jawad. Gets drunk and then decides to play cards with the locals. Loses. Refuses to pay. Now he's missing. With the way that boy was used to mouthing off to people, sooner or later, *something* was going to happen to him. But it will blow over soon enough. Nothing to do with us."

Jawad Sahib's phone rang. He glanced at the screen before shoving it in his pocket.

"Bilal," Jawad Sahib said. "Send my meal to my room."

"Yes, Sahib." He rushed off.

I watched Khan Sahib talk to Nasreen Baji.

There he was—the man I'd heard stories about all my life. The man whose photos lined the hallways I walked through each day. He was the bogeyman our mothers invoked to urge us to finish our dinner. When I was Safa's age, I imagined him to be ten feet tall with beady eyes and pointy teeth. Hafsa was convinced he breathed fire.

But now he stood a few steps away from me. And he didn't breathe fire and he wasn't ten feet tall.

He and Jawad Sahib were powerful and mean-spirited men.

But maybe, just maybe, even they weren't invincible.

Chapter 41

"Jawad Sahib and his father are leaving after dinner tonight," Bilal told me later that afternoon, as we finished cleaning up from lunch. "You should be safe to grab a book if you want to then."

I thanked him and dried my hands before walking over to the servants' verandah. It was empty today. I exhaled and rubbed my temples. Helping Hamid rush to prepare a last-minute lavish lunch for Khan Sahib had left me tired. I wanted to sit down for a moment to catch my breath, but Mumtaz had asked Nabila to clear the teacups from the main verandah, and I knew she was still putting away the dishes from lunch. The sooner we put the house back in order, the sooner *all* of us could rest.

The flowers swayed in the cool afternoon breeze as I strolled through the garden toward the bushes bordering the main verandah. Just then, the sound of voices drifted over to me. I paused by the bushes. They were male voices coming from the other side, steps from where I stood. It had to be Jawad Sahib and his father.

"What did you want me to do?" Jawad argued. "He gambles more than he can pay back and then threatens me? Why should I have been the one to let it go? What is our reputation worth if we take disrespect like that?"

"Well, thanks to you, we now have federal investigators poking their noses in our business," Khan Sahib said.

"They won't find anything! My men took care of it."

"Let's hope you're right for both our sakes."

"I know I'm right. My men enforce all my debts, and they're meticulous. They wouldn't harm the hand that lines their pockets."

"Which one took care of this one?"

"Rehan. I only trusted it to him."

"Tell him to move the body farther out after the investigation dies down. I'm not comfortable with it so close to home."

Their voices stopped.

A door opened and shut in the distance.

Tightness squeezed my chest. I knew Jawad Sahib's

men threatened people and destroyed property. But they killed people? Fozia had said one of his officers was demanding more money. Was this the danger she faced if she couldn't pay?

I backed away from the bushes. Only then did I realize I wasn't alone.

Nabila was staring at me. Her expression was somber.

"Nabila," I began. How much had she heard?

She shook her head furiously and pressed a finger to her mouth.

"Don't say a word," she whispered, gesturing to the balconies and windows all around us. "You never know who is listening."

Chapter 42

"Nabila is acting strange," Mumtaz said to me that evening.

"What do you mean?"

"She didn't eat lunch. Caught her wandering the servants' quarters a little while ago. She was crying. Won't tell me what it is."

"I'll talk to her," I offered.

I walked down to the servants' quarters and peeked into each half-opened room until at last I found her. She was sitting cross-legged on her bed, studying her nails. I took in the dirty concrete floor, the cracked walls.

This was the room I might have had.

"We need to talk," I said.

"Not now," she whispered without looking up. "Jawad and his father are leaving tonight. Meet me and Bilal in the library after everyone is asleep."

Nabila and Bilal were already in the library when I managed to sneak out of Nasreen Baji's room. The room was dark, lit only by the glow of a small desk lamp.

When I closed the door behind me, Nabila walked over to the window and lifted a small ceramic pot resting on the sill. She stuck a finger into the dirt and pulled out a key.

"Nabila, this isn't a good idea," Bilal said.

"I have to know," she told him. She turned and handed me the key. "Please. I need your help. He keeps the debts people owe him filed in there." She pointed to the filing cabinets. "Everything everyone owes him can be found in those cabinets. Can you see if the name Latif is in there? Babar Latif."

"Do you think he borrowed money?"

"Knowing him, yes," she said.

"Nabila . . ." Bilal sighed.

"I know," Nabila said. "But I have to find out."

I turned the key in the first silver cabinet and went through the files. When I tried the next one, I saw his name.

"It's here." I pulled it out and showed her.

"What does it say?" she asked. A tear slipped down her cheek. Bilal put an arm around her.

"He borrowed some money." I scanned the handwritten notes. "Gambling debts. A loan for a motorcycle. The records stop about four or five months ago."

"Makes sense; he's been dead five months."

"Oh, Nabila." I lowered the folder. "Was he a relative?"

"My cousin. He was the only one who never forgot me, who checked in on me and made sure I was okay. He was the sweetest person I knew. They found his body in the fields not far from here. He had just come to see me that morning." Her voice cracked. "Well, at least now I know what happened."

"I'm so sorry, Nabila."

Her face crumpled. Her body was wracked with sobs. She didn't push me away when I put my arms around her.

"Why'd you have to find out?" Bilal kicked the filing cabinet. "I told you not to. You hurt yourself for no reason. It's not like knowing what happened changes anything."

There it was again. Nothing would change.

This family was so powerful, there was no use in trying to fight them. But . . .

"Just because something seems impossible, does that mean we just don't try?" I asked.

They both turned to look at me.

"Try what?" Bilal asked. "There's nothing we can do. No one will do anything about it."

"But what if *we* could do something?" I said. "What if we at least tried to stop him?"

"How?" Nabila brushed away her tears.

"What if we told someone what we heard—told them we know they killed that diplomat's son. Maybe then something would happen."

"Right." Nabila sniffed. "They'll take our word over theirs."

She was right. What reason would anyone have to believe us?

Bilal cleared his throat then.

"What if it wasn't just our word?" he said quietly. "What if we could tell them where the body was?"

"Oh, Bilal," Nabila whispered.

"As his personal servant, I know more than I wish I did." He studied the ground. "He buried the guy by the third tree past the sign for Minawala."

We fell silent for a moment.

"But who do we tell this to?" Nabila asked. "Mumtaz would kill us if she knew we were even talking about something like this."

"I know someone," I said. "My teacher. His father is a lawyer. He'll know who to get the information to."

I said it with such conviction, I almost believed myself. The truth was I had no idea if a lawyer could help us or if Asif would agree in the first place. But I knew I had to try.

If everyone decided nothing could change, nothing ever would.

Chapter 43

Nasreen Baji and Jawad Sahib sat at the dining table eating breakfast. Mumtaz brought out fresh parathas and a plate of softened butter. Everything was normal. It was an ordinary morning. I reminded myself of this.

Nabila placed a glass of orange juice next to Nasreen Baji's plate and a glass next to Jawad Sahib. He talked with his mother. He needed new suits. The gray one looked worn.

After they finished their meals, Jawad Sahib yawned.

"No chai for me today." He rubbed his eyes. "I'm taking a quick nap."

"You see?" Nasreen Baji admonished him. "You work too hard. One can't be up at all hours and expect not to be affected."

I gathered the dishes to take to the kitchen. I washed up the pots and pans and dried my hands. I picked up my satchel and headed to Ghulam's waiting car.

I hurried down the narrow corridor toward Asif's classroom. He was at his desk sorting through papers when I stepped inside.

"I need your help," I said. I tried to stay steady, but everything was catching up to me. The room spun.

Asif took my arm and helped me to a chair. "Take a deep breath. Okay, good. Now tell me. What's wrong?"

I hadn't planned to blurt out everything. But the words wouldn't stop flowing. About the officers. The body. The threats to my neighbors.

When I finished, I caught my breath. Asif's face had gone pale.

"I'm sorry. I shouldn't burden you with this," I said.

"Don't apologize. I'm glad you told me."

"The third tree past the sign for Minawala." My voice wavered. "That's where the body is buried. At least I hope it's still there. I thought maybe you or your father could share that information wherever it needs to go. He's a lawyer, you said?"

Asif stared at me, and then he rested his elbows on the

table and rubbed his temples. "Sharing this with my father doesn't mean anything will actually happen, but if word gets out that they are on to a body, Jawad might hear. There's a chance he could tie it to me, which could lead to you."

"Oh," I said. "I didn't even think of that."

"You live in that house, Amal. If he finds out, it could be bad for you."

I thought of Hazarabad and the burned fields. The charred orange groves. I thought of Fozia.

"It's worth the risk," I said.

"I'll call my father," he said. "I'll see what he says."

"Thank you, Asif. I'm forever indebted to you."

"There's no debt, Amal." He studied me for a moment. "I'm not sure I've ever met anyone as brave as you," he finally said.

"I'm not brave. I'm terrified. I just don't have a choice."

"You always have a choice. Making choices even when they scare you because you know it's the right thing to do—that's bravery."

Chapter 44

Nasreen Baji spoke with her son about marriage prospects over breakfast.

"She comes from a good family," Nasreen Baji told him. "Pretty, too. What harm is there in meeting her? And her father is in politics also. Who knows where it could lead?"

"I thought I'm supposed to celebrate my life in exile here?" He snorted. "No politics for me. I'm doing the most important job there is."

"Jawad, you're twenty-four years old. Enough with the sarcasm already."

"I've met four girls this month alone. It's not my fault none of them is adequate."

"Listen, we both know what this is about." She lowered

her voice. "It's past time to move on. You'll find someone else you like just as much, but only if you give them a chance."

Jawad Sahib looked down at the table.

"Fine," he finally said. "I'll meet her."

I took in the scene before me. Mother and son chatting. Servants picking up empty bowls and dishes, while others brought in white creamy kheer with crushed pistachios. The scent of brewing chai enveloped the room each time the kitchen doors parted.

It had been almost a week since I last saw Asif. Every day I waited for a knock on the door, a phone call, a look of fear across Jawad Sahib's face.

But nothing happened.

Everything continued just as it always had.

My hands shook. I stepped into the hallway to compose myself.

Fatima approached me. "I'm making up my own story tonight," she said. "Baba got me some paper and a freshly sharpened pencil. I'm naming one of the girls after you! It was supposed to be a surprise, but I couldn't wait! But I need your help writing it. I'll do all the pictures. Will you help me when we're done here?"

"Sure." I nodded at the right moments as she explained her story.

Maybe the Khan family really was untouchable.

Nothing had happened to them. Maybe nothing ever would. They had ruled this village for centuries. His mother would take him to meet a prospective bride today. Soon, Jawad would marry. He would have a child, and that child would grow up to rule my village.

Did I really think we could undo it all?

"You're not listening," Fatima sang out to me. "Why are you always thinking? It's good to listen, too."

"Sorry," I said. "After we clean up from breakfast, I'm all yours."

A doorbell chimed in the distance. Then, a hard-knuckled knock.

I walked into the dining room as Jawad Sahib wiped his hands on a napkin and tossed it on a plate.

"The police?" his mother asked.

"Who else?"

"How long will they be?" Nasreen Baji looked at her watch. "We're leaving to meet the girl and her family in an hour, remember?"

"I'll get them out of here in a few minutes."

Footsteps echoed off the foyer.

And then—

I heard Jawad Sahib protest.

Then I heard him yelling and swearing.

I rushed into the hallway. Fatima trailed behind me. Nasreen Baji's face was paper white. There were three officers here. New ones.

And they were slapping handcuffs onto Jawad Sahib's wrists.

"This is a mistake," Jawad Sahib screamed. "My father will speak to you. He won't forget your names."

"We imagine so," one of them said. "We brought him in a few hours ago for questioning."

Upon hearing this, Nasreen Baji started shouting at the officers. She threatened them. She begged them. They didn't respond. It was as if she didn't exist.

Bilal stood to the side, his back pressed against the wall. Other servants gathered in the foyer. Mumtaz rushed over to comfort Nasreen Baji.

I stared at the open door, the empty space through which they marched Jawad Sahib.

It happened.

Jawad Sahib had been arrested.

Chapter 45

The television buzzed low in the background of Nasreen Baji's bedroom. It had now been four days since Jawad Sahib was taken away. At first, Nasreen Baji turned on the television news each morning as though she hoped they would report it all as a big misunderstanding. But once the detectives came and carted away all the silver files—the ones with the debts he and his family collected from everyone in our villages—she stopped hoping.

It was still strange to see Jawad Sahib's face all over the news.

But even stranger was seeing my little village—which didn't even register as a dot on a map—no longer quite so forgotten. This morning, the camera panned to show our rivers, fields, orange groves, and green stalks of sugarcane. The newscaster on the television reported on the changing times and the uprooting of the status quo.

The newspapers Nasreen Baji left lying on the nightstand all echoed the same.

The Crumbling of the Feudal Era

Local Landlord Overthrown

How One Man's Ego Led to His Family's Downfall

The media tied the leaked information to a local officer who claimed responsibility at a press conference, in front of dozens of microphones. I recognized him immediately as the mustached officer who came into the estate months earlier. He was going to be one of the many star witnesses in Jawad Sahib's trial.

I glanced at Nasreen Baji. She stared at the screen; her eyes were red and her cheeks were blotchy. It was as if the contours of her face had changed overnight.

I was glad her son could not hurt anyone ever again,

but seeing Nasreen Baji's grief and knowing her pain was partly because of me made me feel an odd sort of guilt. It was the strangest thing to hold such different feelings inside myself at once.

And as much as Nasreen Baji's life had changed, mine hadn't. Jawad Sahib's arrest didn't mean I could just leave. My debt didn't vanish when the officers carted the silver filing cabinets away. I lived here. And I still washed dishes and helped with dinner. I still brought in fresh flowers and gave the linens to the cleaning girl. I still massaged Nasreen Baji's head and drew her bath.

Everything had changed for so many people, but for me, nothing really had.

"I'll get your breakfast, Nasreen Baji." I brought her tissues from the dresser. She took one and wiped her eyes. She didn't respond.

I went into the kitchen and filled the percolator with water.

"Add some more water for me?" Mumtaz asked. She stood to the side, her shoulders hunched. Toqir and Ghulam were there, too. Toqir pulled out cups from the servants' cupboard and poured in water.

"Are you okay, Mumtaz?" I asked her. "You look pale."

"How can I be okay?" She shook her head.

"Everything is a mess," Toqir agreed. He took a sip of water. "Been here forty years. Never thought I'd see the day."

"But if he did the things the news said he did"—I hesitated—"isn't it a good thing that he's been caught?"

"With the two of them behind bars, what happens to us?" Ghulam asked. "I need this job. My son's wife is about to have a baby. My other grandchild needs to see a specialist in Lahore for his heart. What are we going to do without my income?"

I added an extra cup of water to the percolator and glanced out the window. Other servants were standing outside. I imagined their discussions were the same as the ones in this kitchen. The conversations had run in a loop since that day: Would they really convict him? And what did this mean for us?

I thought Jawad Sahib's arrest would be good for everyone, but it turned out change, no matter how good and necessary, came with a price.

Nabila and Bilal weren't anywhere to be seen. The three of us hadn't talked about what happened since the arrest, afraid to say a word in case someone overheard us, but I walked into the servants' quarters. The tinny sound of the television news echoed in the hallway. Bilal's door was open wide, but Nabila's was closed.

I tapped on it before opening it. Both of them were inside. Bilal stood against the back wall, his arms crossed. Nabila was on her bed, staring at yesterday's discarded newspaper. Grim-faced black-and-white photos of Khan Sahib and Jawad Sahib's faces were front and center.

"I'd ask you to read it to me, but I think I know what it says," she said without looking up.

"It's more of the same," I agreed. "They found the body. Right where he said it was."

"So many reporters outside," Bilal said. "There are even more today than yesterday. They'd climb in through one of the windows here if we didn't have the guards and the brick walls around this place . . ."

Nabila looked up at Bilal and then at me. "Do you think he's gone for good?"

"I hope so," I said.

"It just doesn't feel real." Nabila shook her head. "I still feel like I'll wake up tomorrow and find out it was all a dream."

Nabila was right. It *did* feel surreal. But I glanced at the newspaper in her lap. The black-and-white photos looking back at me were proof it wasn't a dream. After all the people he had hurt, after the generations this family had haunted, we helped bring Jawad Sahib and his father to justice.

I smiled.

No one here except the three of us would ever know it was a group of servants who brought this family down.

No one would ever know it was a girl who helped save our villages.

But I knew.

Chapter 46

"Amal, I need to talk to you," Nasreen Baji said to me the next week. She patted the space on her bed, motioning for me to join her.

"I'm going to Islamabad for a little while," she said when I sat down. "My eldest is coming to get me tomorrow morning. It's too hard to be here right now. This house is too big for me."

My heart sank. Islamabad was hours from here. As her maidservant, I would be expected to go with her. Even farther from my family and all I knew.

"That's good," I managed to say. "It's important to be with your loved ones, especially right now."

"I'm off to see my sister in a little bit—before I go." She smiled at me. It was the first smile since Jawad Sahib had left.

"She will be happy to see you," I told her.

"I hope so," she said, twisting the edge of her scarf. "It's been a long time."

"It's never too late to see your family."

"You're right. And you should be with your family, too."

I looked at her with a start.

"You may as well hear it from me first. There's no use in keeping everyone on while we wait to see what happens. I'm closing up the house. Mumtaz will come with me to Islamabad, of course, and a few people, like the gardener, will stay on here to take care of the estate. But most everyone else will be let go."

"You're . . . you're going to let me go?"

"I thought about keeping you." She smiled at me sadly. "I've enjoyed your company and have grown fond of you. I see in you so much the girl I was. But you belong with your family. Your debt is forgiven."

I wanted to hug Nasreen Baji, but I had never embraced her before. Whatever spell she was under, whatever sacred moment this was, I didn't want to risk breaking it.

"Thank you," I whispered.

• • •

Later that afternoon, I sat with the others as Nasreen Baji shared what was to come.

Bilal's face broke open with disbelief and then widened into a smile. Hamid hugged Fatima. But Ghulam was somber. And when I looked at Mumtaz, she was crying.

"But you're going to stay on." I walked over and clasped her hands. "You're going to her home in Islamabad."

"But *this* was *my* home." She looked up at me. "Take care of yourself and check in on an old lady now and then, if you can?" she said through her tears.

"I will." I hugged her. I felt surprised by the sadness overtaking me. I had waited so long for this day, and I was glad to leave, but I *would* miss Mumtaz and the other servants.

Fatima approached me a little while after. She held Hamid's hand. "We're leaving. My parents don't want me. Baba said I can go home with him."

"Where are you going?" I asked Hamid.

"Back home," he said. "Imrawala. Wife and children are waiting. Have been for too long. Have a couple of grandkids Fatima's age." He looked down at Fatima and smiled. "It will be nice for you to have some children to play with."

Fatima's eyes watered when I walked over to her. She was my first friend here, the person who gave me a chance before anyone else would.

"When you finish writing your story, will you send it to me?" I asked her. "I want to read it."

She looked at the ground and didn't respond.

"We'll see each other at the market. Hamid's village is just on the other side from where I live. I'll find you. We'll stay in touch," I promised.

"But it won't be the same," she whispered.

"No," I told her. "It won't be the same. But maybe it will be better."

She hugged me. I watched her follow Hamid out the door, out of sight.

I picked up my satchel and felt a tap. Nabila.

"Here." She pushed a cloth bag toward me. "I packed some snacks for you. Some water. In case you need it for the walk home."

"Where are you going?" I asked her. "Back home?"

"No. Never. I'm going to live with my cousin Latif's wife in my old village near Simranwala. She needs all the help she can get."

"You going back to school?" I asked her.

"I'm not sure." She shrugged.

"The literacy center is free, Nabila. I really liked it, and it's not far from where you'll be. Give it a chance. We might even bump into each other—it's just around the corner from where I live."

"Maybe. And you *better* go back to school. You have to become a teacher. It's not every day you get a second chance like this."

"I hope so." I smiled.

I could hardly believe there was a time she was anything but a friend to me. I leaned over and embraced her.

I pulled my suitcase behind me as dusk settled. A crescent moon was etched into the sky above. Soon stars would glitter overhead. But I didn't need them to guide me. I knew my way home. I thought about what Nabila had said. Maybe I *would* be a teacher one day. Or maybe I'd write a book. Or set up schools, like Asif. Or maybe I would do all these things. I knew now that one person could hold many different dreams and see them all come true. And one was coming true right now. I was leaving this estate behind me.

The walk took longer than I thought. I kept expecting someone to come after me. To snatch me away and take me back to the estate. But no one came.

I kept walking. Each step took me closer to my parents, to Seema and Omar and Hafsa. I didn't look back. I followed the winding path, walking over potholes, some so deep they seemed to crack open into the center of the earth.

I wondered what would happen next.

Would Jawad Sahib be released one day? Would he come searching for me?

I thought not knowing would scare me, but I didn't feel afraid. Today I was free, and even if I didn't know what the future held, I knew I was going home.

And right now, in this moment, this was enough.

Author's Note

In 2012, Malala Yousafzai was on her way home from school in the Swat Valley region of Pakistan when she was shot at point-blank range. Her crime? Malala wanted an education, and she regularly spoke out against people who opposed her right to do so.

When Malala was attacked, people from around the world stopped and paid attention, and when she recovered, they rooted for her as she renewed her quest for an education not just for herself, but for all girls. Malala continues to embody what it means to be a strong girl. She builds schools, advocates against violence, and is the youngest recipient of the Nobel Peace Prize. Children around the world know her story.

Malala is truly brave, but even she acknowledges that she is one of many young people all over the world who fight for what they believe in, who do the right thing even when it is difficult, even when the risks are overwhelming. Most of these people will never get a headline in the newspaper, we will never know who they are, and sadly, most of them will not get the type of happy ending Malala has, but they are still brave and courageous and worthy of respect, whether a spotlight shines on them or not.

Amal is a fictional character, but she represents countless other girls in Pakistan and around the world who take a stand against inequality and fight for justice in often unrecognized but important ways. We don't have to make headlines to help change the world for the better. Everything we do in our communities and beyond to impart good is important and matters.

The issue of indentured servitude covered in this book is a global problem affecting millions of people, including in the United States. While some experience situations similar to Amal's, unfortunately, the vast majority suffer much more difficult situations with no end in sight. Amal's reality is far luckier than most who endure this horrendous practice.

There are brave girls all over the world. They may feel afraid sometimes, like Amal. But doing the right thing despite the risks it may involve is the bravest thing there can be. It is my hope this story shines a light on brave girls everywhere.

Acknowledgments

This book wouldn't have been possible without the support of my amazing agent, Taylor Martindale Kean. Many thanks to Stefanie Von Borstel and the entire team at Full Circle Literary. Thank you to Nancy Paulsen for understanding the heart of the story I wanted to tell and helping me realize it—I am inordinately blessed. Thank you to Sara LaFleur for all your feedback and insight, as well as a huge thanks to the entire team at Penguin Young Readers: this book wouldn't have been possible without all of you, and I am grateful for each and every one of you. Thank you to Shezil Malik for a cover that captures the heart of this book.

To Tracy Lopez and Emily Pan: thanks for being the

best critique partners I could ask for. Many thanks to Saira Adeel, Bakhat Nazir, and Attiya Nazir for your feedback on earlier drafts of this book. Thank you to Saadia Memon, Nigar Haroon, Becky Albertalli, Ayesha Mattu, Aamina Amin, and Ali and Aamir Saeed for the emotional support along the writing journey.

Thank you to my parents not only for your invaluable input, but for always being proud of me. Zayn, Musa, and Waleed: the three of you are the light of my life. And finally, to Kashif Iqbal—the best thing that ever happened to me. No book would be possible without you. I love you more than I can say.